THE FUGITIVE HEIR

Matt & Michelle Book 1

HENRY VOGEL

Published in the United States of America by Rampant Loon Press, an imprint of Rampant Loon Media LLC, P.O. Box 111, Lake Elmo, Minnesota 55042. "Rampant Loon Press" and the Rampant Loon colophon are trademarks of Rampant Loon Media LLC.

www.rampantloonmedia.com

Cover design by goonwrite.com

ISBN: 978-1-938834-66-0 (ebook)

ISBN: 978-1-938834-67-7 (print)

First publication: February 2016

For Audrey, the Michelle of my life.

MEMORIAL SERVICE

"My parents are not dead!"

Like a pebble dropped into a placid pond, my words sent a ripple of agitation from the front pew of the packed cathedral to the rear. Sitting right below my position in the pulpit, Aunt Tess buried her face in her hands. Next to her, Uncle Gunther met my eyes and slowly shook his head.

Feeling a pang of guilt at the looks on their faces, I reached out with my power. As always, I felt Mom's and Dad's presence—far, far away but as warm and alive as always. If I lived in a different galaxy and under a different government, I could just announce what my power told me. In this galaxy and under this government, such a claim would mean impressment into Psi Corps, the loss of my freedom, and the loss of any hope I had of finding my parents. With no other way to get my parents back, I forged on with my plan.

"I *know* my parents have been missing for seven years. I *know* there's never been an attempt to collect a ransom. I *know* my parents' spaceship has never been found. I *know* none of you believe me. I *know* you all think I should just shut up and be the spoiled rich kid the public already thinks I am."

I paused and let my gaze wander over the crowd once again

still as that placid pond. Their faces displayed stern disapproval, horrified fascination, and consternation. The few newsies covering the service radiated excited anticipation as I turned a boring obit story into a juicy scandal.

"And I *know* my parents still live." I returned my gaze to my aunt and uncle, the only family I'd known for the past seven years. "Uncle Gunther, I'm sorry to ruin the memorial service you worked so hard on. Aunt Tess, I'm sorry to revive the pain you felt when your brother—my father—went missing. Truly, I am. But I cannot simply stand before all of these people and pretend they are dead." I gave my uncle a half-smile. "You hate yes men, Uncle Gunther. Would you have me become one? Would you have me go along to get along?"

Shaking my head, I climbed down from the pulpit and paced before the men and women in the front pew, members of the GenCo board of directors. One by one, I met and held their eyes. One by one, each member of the board turned away from my gaze.

"For the last several months, you members of the board have sidled up to me and, when no one else was around, asked what I would do with my inheritance." I stopped, straightened my shoulders, and deepened my voice to mimic the voices of the older men before me. "You're going to be the richest person on the planet, Matt, but you're still young. You should be busy enjoying your youth—spending time in the company of pretty girls or hoisting a few beers with friends while arguing the fate of galactic civilization or something else wild and crazy. You know, doing all those things we old folks tsk about but secretly wish we could do. You shouldn't be worrying about the responsibilities of running an interstellar corporation. There will be plenty of time for that when you're old and set in your ways, like me. Have you thought about which board member will best represent your interests, son? Have you thought about who you'll assign your proxies to?"

I returned to my normal voice. "I won't insult the ladies on the board by attempting to mimic their voices. Their message was couched in maternal phrases about finding the right girl and settling down, but the rest was essentially the same."

I laughed and shook my head and paced a little more. I looked at the floor, not the crowd, but my voice carried easily over my silent audience.

"By an amazing coincidence, each of you did your best to convince me that you deserved to hold my proxies. My, but you certainly are a caring lot, each of you angling to convince me you're my friend, my buddy, my pal. But none of you ever mentioned the one thing I care the most about. Not one of you mentioned helping me search for my parents."

I ascended into the pulpit once more and looked down on the front pew from on high.

"Well, ladies and gentlemen, I listened to what each of you said. I carefully considered everything each of you told me. And you'll be happy to hear that your touching concern for me was invaluable helping me decide the best way to use that fortune I'll inherit in three days."

I placed my hands on the edge of the pulpit and leaned forward, just like a priest driving home the message from a sermon.

"Ladies and gentlemen, I am going to liquidate my entire inheritance. Then, I am going to use that money. To. Find. My. Parents."

Shouts of outrage and alarm rose from the crowd, most especially the members of the board sitting before me. I ignored them, descended from the pulpit, and left the sanctuary by the priest's entrance at the front of the cathedral.

My bodyguard fell in beside me as I exited the sanctuary. I didn't tell him I was coming out this way and it impressed me that he figured it out so quickly. So much for a few minutes of solitude after my speech.

"May I offer a comment, sir?"

"I'm surprised you asked, Jonas. Usually, you just go ahead and give your blunt assessment of my incautious behavior."

"Speaking at your parents' memorial service is bound to be

emotionally trying, sir. My observations can wait if you want time to regain your equilibrium."

"Did you listen to my speech, Jonas?"

"I noted it while watching for threats, sir."

"Then you know I believe my parents are still alive. Don't you think that would immunize me against such emotions?"

"Not necessarily, sir. I imagine the impact is different than mourning the dead, but knowing others do not believe as you do must be emotionally draining, as well."

Jonas knew me well. He had been with me since before my parents disappeared so that's not a surprise. The depth of his insight *was* a surprise.

"After seven years of disbelief, I barely notice that drain on my emotions. Speak your piece."

"You should not have announced your intention to liquidate your inheritance until the liquidation was in process. You've told some of the richest, most powerful people on Draconis that you are a threat to their way of life. It was not one of your better moves."

I have never been called an idiot quite so politely, but I cringed anyway.

"My apologies, Jonas. I got carried away by the moment."

"No doubt, sir. I do hope the looks on their faces gave you some pleasure. You should get *something* beneficial out of this."

"Oh, it felt great!"

"I further hope that feeling will carry you through the next few days of restricted activity."

I sighed. "You're going to tell Uncle Gunther to keep me inside the house until he can try to talk me out of this."

"I am, sir. It's for your own protection. Now, am I correct in assuming you will be skipping the reception after the memorial service?"

"You are. I have no interest in being lectured by every member of the board."

4

"Very good, sir. I ordered the car brought to the rear exit before you finished your speech."

———

Jonas offered his suggestion and my uncle readily acceded to it. It's amazing how confining a five thousand square meter house and a ten square kilometer lawn can feel when you are not allowed to leave them.

To my surprise, neither my uncle nor aunt tried to talk me out of my plans. Instead, they were *understanding*. It was an insidious plan on their part and, despite my best intentions, by the second day my determination to liquidate my inheritance began to waver. I had to get out of the house and regain my perspective.

There was one place I always went when I needed to think things over. I went to the docking bay where Dad and I kept our rebuilt spaceship. The two of us had spent hundreds of hours working on the ship when I was growing up. After Dad and Mom disappeared, I always felt closest to them when I was tinkering on the spaceship.

My bodyguards knew this. When they discovered I had slipped away, they would know exactly where to find me. But that was okay. Just one hour alone on the little spaceship would restore my crumbling willpower.

All I had to do was fool a team of the best bodyguards money could buy and slip away. Not an easy task, but I've been doing it off and on for years. I'm quite good at it. Of course, the bodyguards are quite good at countering my escape attempts. But this time I had a surprise I'd held in reserve for over a year, something my bodyguards would never suspect until it was too late.

As darkness fell, I turned on the shower in my suite, running the water good and hot to mask me from the house's thermal sensors. The bodyguards wouldn't worry because the sensors would pick me up again before I even left the bathroom. Except the sensors would *not* pick me up. Standing next to the shower, I pulled on my little surprise—a military-grade thermal dampening suit.

GenCo, my father's company—my company, by this time tomorrow—made the suits and I'd managed to get my hands on one. In truth, I'd gotten my hands on the components for the suit and spent close to six months assembling it. It was time to find out if my suit worked or not.

I activated the suit and left the bathroom. Crossing to my balcony, I slid down a rope to the ground fifteen meters below. I stole across the lawn, flitting from shadow to shadow. No floodlights came on. No alarms sounded. Five minutes later, I was over the wall and gliding past neighboring mansions and away into the night.

I'd done it. For an hour or two, I was free and clear.

A NEAR ESCAPE

Getting over the wall and away from the house was only part of the challenge. I was still a long way from the center-city docking bay that was home to my spaceship. Most days, a couple of bodyguards drove me to the site. Sometimes I drove myself, closely followed by a car carrying two or three bodyguards. For obvious reasons, both of those options were out. So I did what no one would expect.

I took public transport.

It was a short walk to the local maglev station; the help has to get to and from their jobs in the mansions somehow after all. A couple of minutes later, I caught the first train back to the city. The half full train carried me through a dozen stations, the crowd ebbing and flowing around me. No one bothered me, leaving me alone with my thoughts.

Ten minutes from my stop, my comm buzzed. I'd brought one of several unlisted and unregistered comms I owned. It's amazing what you can get away with when you own the company. In other words, no one should have this comm code. Certain it could only be a wrong number, I let it go to the message bank.

Within seconds, the comm buzzed again. Irritated, I waited for it to go to the message bank again.

"Idiot! Listen to the comm message before calling again. You've got a wrong number."

Based on the vids I watched, people on trains talked to themselves all the time. Based on the looks I got from people nearby, reality was different.

I gave a sheepish smile to the nearest passenger. "Sorry. Someone keeps calling and they never leave a message."

"Then why don't you answer it and tell the person of their error?" The passenger, a middle-aged woman, shook her head in disapproval. "The caller could be flustered due to an emergency, have coded the comm wrong the first time, and keep hitting the repeat button. Young people today have no manners. I'd never have ignored a comm when *I* was your age."

I pulled the comm out of my pocket. "Thank you, ma'am. I hadn't considered that and will remember what you've told me."

That earned me a slight smile and a nod. The woman turned back to her reader.

I thumbed the comm and, in case the woman was still listening, adopted my polite young man voice.

"I'm sorry, I don't recognize your comm code. I believe you may have miscoded."

The woman's smile widened. She *had* been listening.

"Where are you, sir?"

"*Jonas?*"

"You're not the only person with unlisted comms, sir."

"Apparently my comms aren't as unlisted as I thought. How did you get this code?"

"There's a record for every comm code, even unlisted ones. And your uncle is chairman of the board of the conglomerate that manufactured your comm."

We pulled up to the last station before my exit. Almost everyone got off at this stop, including Miss Manners. She gave me a little wave which I returned.

"As I asked before, sir, where are you?"

"I'm on the maglev train, heading to the docks in the center of town."

"How many stations are left before you reach the docks?"

"We just pulled away from the last station."

"Can you look about your car without appearing to do so, sir?"

It was dark outside the car and well-lit inside. I could easily see the interior of the car reflected in the windows. I didn't know what had Jonas so worried until I saw the reflection of the six men about my own age sitting a few rows behind me.

"There are eight other people in the car. Two men sitting by themselves and six guys about my age in the back of the car. The six guys keep looking my way."

"Do you see a transit officer or a more crowded car?"

I looked up through moving tunnel of linked cars and back through the reflections.

"No to both, Jonas. Suggestions?"

"Are you armed?"

"It's against the law to bring weapons on public transport."

"Next time you pull a stunt like this, please disregard such laws. I'd much rather deal with the police than the coroner."

"I'm glad you think there will be a next time, Jonas."

"I will get you out of this, sir, if for no other reason than the pleasure I will take from giving you a verbal flaying. Back to the matter at hand. Is anyone in the car ahead of you?"

"Three people, all older, none together."

"Good. Stay in your seat until the train begins slowing for the next station. Rise slowly, as if you're just another traveler getting off the train. At the last second, bolt for the next car and out its door."

"Got it. What then?"

"The platform exit will be to the right. Head out onto the street and turn left. Watch for an oh six green Jusair. The driver is one of us."

"That car is older than me, Jonas. Are you-"

"Pay attention to the situation, sir, not the year the car was built. Is the station in sight?"

"Yes."

"Then it's time to put away the comm and concentrate on the plan."

As much as I wanted to get away from Jonas and the others earlier, I no longer wanted to be alone.

"Jonas, does this have anything to do with my announcement?"

"Of course."

"I'm scared."

"I know you are, sir. And, if I may be allowed to say, it's about damned time."

Despite myself, I gave a short laugh.

"I'll talk to you soon, sir."

Standing as the train slowed, I pocketed the comm unit. My eyes flicked to the reflection in the windows. The six guys in the rear stood, all of them openly eying me. I lifted my arms as if stretching. The guys in the back grinned at each other, thinking I would be an easy mark.

I broke off my stretch and sprinted for the next car. Shouts erupted behind me, followed by the clatter of footsteps as the gang came after me.

The train slowed to a crawl as it pulled up to the station. Between me and the door, an older man rose to his feet and turned toward the aisle.

"Watch out, sir!"

The man started at my shout and looked at me. His eyes widened, and he slumped back into his seat. Fearful eyes tracked me as I dashed past him.

I turned my attention to the still-closed door. Should I hope the door opened in time or run to the next car? A glance toward the next car showed a pair of young guys blocking the aisle. Great, the gang behind me had friends in front of me.

The door hissed and began opening when I was five meters away. Never had a door moved so slowly. I turned sideways and slipped through the partially open door. A hand snatched at my sleeve, but I pulled it free and ran to the right, just as Jonas instructed.

Two of my pursuers slid through the door like I had, but the others piled up against the slow-moving barrier. At least I'd managed to put a few more meters between me and most of them.

I dodged around a few people, all of whom shrank back as I passed. From their reactions, I guessed this kind of thing wasn't as unusual to them as it was to me.

I reached the escalator down to street level. The stairs were not moving, but I had never considered simply riding the thing down, anyway. I hit the stairs and leapt down five steps. More people trudged down the stairs ahead of me, blocking my way.

Leaping another five steps, I shouted, "Get out of the way!"

Most of the people scooted to the right side of the motionless stairs without looking back, but one man refused to move. His shoulders stiffened at my shout, so he had heard me. I guess he was just tired of young punks ordering him around. I sympathized —I really did—but his stubborn reaction might get me killed.

Thanking the education gods that gymnastics was still a sport taught in expensive private schools, I brought both feet together and jumped from three steps above the stubborn man. Tucking, I used the man's shoulders as a vault. He shouted in surprise when I flipped from his shoulders. I unfolded from the tuck and prepared for a blind landing. You always land blind after a forward flip and I could only guess how far I had to fall to reach the ground. I guessed wrong.

My right ankle twisted beneath me as I hit the floor at the bottom of the escalator. I went limp and rolled, trying to save my ankle from a sprain or break. Pain blossomed from the ankle as I came to my feet. Ignoring the pain, I staggered toward the street just a few meters away.

Shouts of alarm rang behind me as the gang chasing me shoved people out of their way. Limping as fast as I could, I risked a look behind me. The guys closest to me lay tangled among the people they'd barreled into while chasing me. The rest of the gang pounded down the other side of the escalator, people below them jumping out of their way.

Hoping my ankle would hold for a few more seconds and hoping even more that Jonas's associate was on time, I turned left and ran on. Pain lanced through my ankle with every pounding step I took. From the shouts and footsteps behind me, my lead over the gang was no more than five meters.

Shouts of joyous rage rose behind me. "We got you now, punk!"

Powerful repulsers whined behind me, drowning out the shouts. A green Jusair shot across my path and the passenger door flew open.

"Matt, duck!"

The voice was young and feminine and, somehow, familiar.

I dropped and rolled toward the car. The second I was out of the way, a steady stream of blaster bolts flashed over my head. Cries of pain and fear broke from the gang on my heels. The firing stopped as suddenly as it started.

"Get in but stay low!"

I rose to a crouch and dove into the car. The driver put the car into a tight spin and I found my head laying in her lap, a bare midriff right before my eyes. My ankle throbbed, and I had just escaped death by the skin of my teeth, yet my mind focused exclusively on the belly button mere centimeters before my nose.

"Are you okay, Matt?"

The familiar voice drew my attention from my navel gazing. I rolled my head and looked up. The soft glow from the dashboard lit blonde hair framing a very pretty and very familiar face.

"Michelle?"

"Yep. It looks like you've been busy since the semester ended."

I struggled to sit up, but Michelle just pushed my head down into her lap again. I really liked the view from her lap, so didn't struggle.

"Um, not that I'm complaining, Michelle, but what the hell are you doing here?"

"Saving your ass, Matt."

"Yeah, and thanks. Seriously. But I was expecting one of my bodyguards, not someone from school."

Michelle laughed and patted my head. "Silly boy, I *am* one of your bodyguards."

"Since when?"

"Since we first met, back in sixth grade."

Michelle checked her exterior view cams, either oblivious to the bombshell she'd just dropped or pretending to be.

"Okay, you can sit up now."

My mind whirled through school memories before settling down on the day I'd met Michelle. Well, the day I first saw her, anyway. Every boy in our class fell in love with her the first day she came to our school. She wasn't the prettiest girl in school—that title belonged to Jayna, with her best friend Brenda a close second —but Michelle didn't act as if her looks made her some sort of royalty. You never felt Michelle was looking down her nose at you when she talked to you. Unlike many of the other guys in school, I never fell out of love with her.

Michelle spoke again, interrupting my memories. "I said, you can sit up now, Matt."

"Oh! Sorry, Michelle." I sat up. "I was... It's just... You surprised me. I never knew I had a bodyguard *in* my school. Especially one as pretty as you."

Oh, crap, had I just said that out loud?

"I mean, as *young* as you."

Michelle laughed, and it was filled with good humor rather than the scorn I'd expected. She glanced at me, her blue eyes reflecting the same humor I heard in her laugh.

"That's very kind of you to say, Matt."

"Um, that you're pretty? I know you're not blind or stupid, Michelle. You've got to know that already."

"No, it's not that, though it *is* charming the way you just blurted it out."

"Then I really don't understand. Unless you think we're not young."

Michelle patted my leg. "No, it's that you never knew anyone was guarding you inside the school. It means I've done my job well." Like flipping a switch, Michelle was suddenly all business. "And mentioning that job, I need to check in."

She touched a button on the dash and a vid screen sprang to life. Jonas looked out from the screen. His eyes flicked between Michelle and me.

"You're both safe and unharmed, Michelle?"

"I think Matt turned his ankle running from the gang, but otherwise yes to both questions."

"Report."

With an economy of words our literature teacher would have admired, Michelle related her end of the pickup. When she finished, I described what had happened after Jonas signed off and before Michelle arrived.

"Now, Jonas, don't you think you ought to tell me what's going on?"

"Yes, but not over the vid."

"Fine. Michelle can bring me home."

"Good. And we can have your ankle checked when you get here. Michelle-"

"No, I should *not* bring Matt home. There are too many eyes and ears around. Have Matt come home with a girl and I can guarantee some servant will make a few credits selling that information to the newsies."

"Being known as Matt's girlfriend *would* give you a good reason to be by Matt's side at all times."

I liked the sound of that.

"Maybe, but Matt should know everything we know before agreeing to something like that."

Jonas pondered for a moment. "Okay, what do you suggest we do?"

"Meet us at Matt's spaceship. It's where he was going, anyway, and a sealed spaceship is about as safe from attacks and from eavesdroppers as anything we're likely to find."

Jonas bestowed one of his rare smiles on the girl. "Good idea. I'll be there in thirty minutes. Is there anything else?"

"Yes. Call Mom and let her know I'll be home late."

"Will do. See you in thirty."

"Bye, Daddy."

My eyes flicked back and forth between Michelle and the now-blank vid screen and my mouth dropped open.

Michelle giggled, the business-like bodyguard replaced by a young college coed in the blink of an eye. She reached out and gently pushed my mouth shut.

I blame my next statement on the unsettling events of the previous ten minutes.

"How long has Jonas been your father?"

That brought a long, loud laugh from Michelle.

"All of my life, Matt. That's usually how these things work."

I felt the blush rise up my face. God, how could I have said something so stupid to the girl I most wanted to impress?

Michelle reached out to me again and gave my hand a gentle squeeze. "It's okay, Matt. You've had a lot of shocks and surprises tonight. If you ask me, you're holding up really well."

She steered into the docks and found a parking spot close to my ship. When we climbed out, she put an arm around me.

"You're just a guy showing off his spaceship to his new girl, okay?"

I put my arm around Michelle and pulled her close. "Well, if you insist..."

My recent few minutes of sheer terror were all worth it for that short walk to the spaceship. Okay, maybe not entirely worth it, but holding Michelle and feeling the sway of her hips against mine made up for a lot. Inside the spaceship, I actually did show it off to Michelle.

Then Jonas arrived and my life changed forever.

THE REVELATION

Michelle opened the airlock when Jonas arrived. My head of security smiled fondly and gave Michelle a peck on the forehead. She kissed his cheek in return. I found the simple, intimate gesture between father and daughter sweet, painfully so. More than a third of my life had passed since I'd had such a moment with my parents.

Jonas eyed Michelle's short, pleated skirt and bare midriff.

"You wore *that* to a rescue, Michelle?"

Michelle looked my way and rolled her eyes. "No, Daddy, I wore this to a club. Which you called me away from for this rescue."

"A club is worse! What kind of signals do you think that outfit sends in that setting?"

"Maybe that I like to dance?"

"Do you think that's the only message the boys at the club picked up, pumpkin?"

I watched and listened in fascination. I'd never seen this side of Jonas. Heck, I'd never even imagined it existed.

"Daddy, I cannot help what a bunch of stuck up, trust fund boys think when they see me. Besides, I dressed conservatively compared to the other girls." Michelle turned a grin my way. "You should have seen Jayna. She might as well have written 'slut' on her forehead."

"I don't care what your friends wore, Michelle. The point is-"

"Jayna is *not* my friend."

"The *point* is that you know you could get called into work at a moment's notice—like you did tonight. Your clothes must reflect that reality."

Michelle pointed at her shoes, open-toed with flat heels. "I wore sensible shoes, Daddy. And I'll bet you Matt's inheritance that my legs have more range of motion in this skirt than yours do in any pair of pants you own."

I burst out laughing. "She's got you there, Jonas. And you've got to admit she did a great job rescuing me."

Michelle bestowed a bright smile on me. "Thank you, Matt."

My words drew Jonas's attention away from Michelle's clothing and onto me. "You're right on both counts, sir. Now, let me take a look at that ankle."

Jonas poked and prodded for a moment. "It's not broken or sprained. I can give you something for the pain, but there's no need for medical nanites. It will heal by morning."

I waved away the pain med he offered. "I'm worried about my life, Jonas, not my ankle. And I'm worried about Michelle's life and your life and the lives of my other bodyguards. So, what's going on?"

Jonas rose to his feet and started pacing. Since her father needed the meager floor space in the lounge to pace, Michelle came to the couch where I was stretched out. I started to sit up.

"Your ankle should stay elevated, Matt. Just lift your head for a second."

I did and Michelle slid onto the couch beneath my head. It was uncomfortable, holding my head up like that, but I didn't say anything. Then Michelle put her hand on my forehead and pushed my head down onto her lap for the second time that night.

Best. Night. Ever.

"You've already figured out most of it, Matt. One of the major shareholders, probably a member of the board of directors, wants to stop you from liquidating those shares you're set to inherit tomorrow. Your well-known tendency to slip away from your bodyguards' protection gave them hope they could make your death look like random violence."

"What if I had just stayed holed up in the house until it was time to attend the inheritance appointment?"

"I suspect the attack would have been much more public and much more obvious. And a lot more people would have been endangered." Jonas stopped pacing. "It took me a couple of days to put all of this together, sir. Had you not slipped out of the house, I'd be having this discussion with you, your aunt, and your uncle right now. Drastic measures are called for, sir."

That put a damper on the best night ever, even when Michelle began stroking my head in sympathy.

"So you're saying I have to give up my dream of finding my parents and announce it to the public?"

"That would be a start, sir, but I'm afraid it's going to take more than that. To stave off attacks, I strongly recommend that you assign full control of all of your shares to your uncle or some other member of the board."

"Meaning I couldn't vote or sell my shares."

"Yes, sir."

"For how long?"

"I suggest a minimum of seven years."

"And if I don't make the announcement, I die and you and Michelle might get caught in the crossfire?"

"I'm afraid so, sir."

"That is *so* not fair, Daddy!"

"Life isn't fair, pumpkin. You know that."

"Do it." It came out as a harsh whisper.

"Are you certain, sir? I admit I believe it is necessary, but should you choose otherwise I will abide by your decision." Jonas's eyes flicked to Michelle. "I will, of course, take the precaution of removing Michelle from your security detail."

I felt Michelle draw in a breath to protest her father's pronouncement. "That won't be necessary, Jonas. After all, it's not like I really have any other choice."

Jonas sighed and shook his head. "No sir, you don't. Let's get you home and I'll get the announcement out to the board and the newsies."

"Matt should stay clear of his home until the news is out, Daddy. After all, that's where the assassins would expect to find him."

Jonas nodded his head slowly, agreeing with his daughter's assessment. "Where do you suggest I take him, Michelle?"

"Nowhere. Let him spend the night here. At least let him mourn the loss of his dream in the place where he's most comfortable."

Jonas thought for a moment. "I suppose I could send for a couple of bodyguards."

"Matt already has a bodyguard here, Daddy. I'll stay with him."

Jonas' eyebrows climbed to his hairline. In other circumstances, I'd have laughed.

"I've got this, Daddy."

Jonas's fond smile returned. "I guess you do. Okay, pumpkin, I'll call once it's safe for Matt to come out."

Michelle let her father out and sealed the ship's airlock. When she returned, Michelle slid back into her place on the couch, once again resting my head in her lap. She met my gaze, and I saw her blue eyes were bright with unshed tears.

"I can't imagine what you must be feeling right now, Matt, but holding it in won't help."

A single tear spilled from her right eye and rolled down her cheek. With that tear, the dam holding my emotions in check burst.

I buried my head against Michelle and sobbed.

Sometime later, purged of tears and emotion, I fell quiet. Michelle stroked my hair, silently giving comfort and understanding. I wrapped my arms about her waist and gently squeezed, my cheek pressing into her soft stomach.

"Goodbye, Mom. Goodbye, Dad." My ragged whisper blew across Michelle's skin.

I rolled my head and looked up at Michelle. Tear tracks coursed down her cheeks and her eyes still shone with sympathy. She smiled and wiped her cheeks.

"Do you feel better, Matt?"

I took stock and realized I did. "Yes. Thanks for being here for me and thanks for understanding."

"It's okay, Matt. It's hard to give up a cherished belief after so long."

I shook my head. "It's not a belief, Michelle, and I sure as hell am not giving up on it. I do not simply *believe* my parents are alive. I *know* it like I know your eyes are blue."

"I don't understand how, Matt." Her eyes widened. "Unless there was some kind of attempt to ransom them that no one knows about. Is that it? Has someone been holding them for over seven years, waiting for you to inherit your parents' fortune so you could pay the ransom?"

"No, there's never been any attempt to collect a ransom. I've known my parents still lived from the first moment we learned they had disappeared. I will know it for as long as they live."

Michelle shook her head slowly. "That doesn't make any sense, Matt. How could you possibly know something like that?"

For nearly thirteen years—up until their disappearance—my parents drilled into me that I must never tell anyone this secret. Not even Aunt Tess or Uncle Gunther knew. But I wanted Michelle to understand my certainty. After seven years, I wanted to share my secret with someone. After seven years, I wanted to break my silence. But that meant breaking my word to my parents.

My indecision must have been obvious. Michelle took my head between her hands and turned it so our eyes met.

"You can trust me, Matt. Whatever your secret is, I *will* keep it." She flashed a reassuring smile. "You never guessed I was one of your bodyguards, so you know I can keep secrets."

I shut my eyes, afraid to watch Michelle's face as she absorbed my words.

"Michelle, I... I'm psychic." Her body stiffened. "I'm not a very strong psychic. I can only sense close family members when they're nearby and I can do some other little stuff. But I can *always* sense my parents."

There. I'd shared my secret. It was time to discover if I was an idiot or not.

Seconds as long as hours passed in silence before Michelle spoke. "Can you read my thoughts?"

"No, I'm not a telepath. I can sense a person's emotions, but only if the emotions are strong and I'm touching the person. The more intimate the contact, the better my read is." A memory rose, unbidden. "You know, I never doubted my parents' love because I felt waves of it every time we hugged."

"Can you read me, Matt?"

I opened my eyes. "Do you want me to try?"

Michelle nodded, so I put her hand against my cheek and held it there. I calmed my mind, pushing distracting images out of the way and concentrating on Michelle. The gang members faded away. Jonas faded away. Finally, even my agreement to postpone the search for my parents faded away. The feel of Michelle's hand on my cheek possessed my conscious mind. My psychic power rose and read her strongest emotion.

Fear.

I rolled off the couch onto the floor where I curled up in a ball of absolute misery. I'd lost the chance to search for my parents *and* terrified the girl I'd loved ever since I first met her.

"Matt?" Michelle sounded concerned. Was she worried I'd picked up some deep secret or something?

With a thump, Michelle dropped to the floor next to me. Her hands tried to take mine, but I yanked them away.

"What's wrong, Matt? Why are you acting this way?"

"Isn't it obvious? I don't want to *inflict* myself on you, Michelle."

"What are you talking about?"

"Oh, come on! I told you I only read strong emotions. Did you think I wouldn't pick up that emotion?"

"*Which* emotion, Matt?"

"I know you're scared of me, Michelle. You broadcast fear loud and clear."

Michelle blew out her breath in exasperation. "Matthew Bernard Connaught, sit up and look at me."

Her tone of voice reminded me so much of my mother that I found myself obeying without conscious thought. Her blue eyes burned with an intensity I'd never seen before.

"You said intimate contact makes someone easier for you to read?"

"Yes."

Michelle drew me close and kissed me—and I'm not talking about a simple peck on the lips. The kiss was long and sensuous and exactly the kind of kiss I'd always fantasized having with her. Her lips parted and her tongue flicked against mine. I pulled her to me, one hand on the small of her back, the other behind her head.

Michelle broke our lip lock, but stayed close enough that her lips brushed mine when she spoke. "Read me *now*."

Then her lips met mine again and drew me back into my fantasy kiss. I felt Michelle's body moving against mine. I tasted her lips. I smelled her perfume. I heard her panting breath. She consumed my senses, driving everything else from my mind. And, just like that, her strongest emotions blazed forth with a brilliance I'd never experienced before.

Michelle wasn't afraid *of* me. She was afraid *for* me. I broke the kiss and stared at her in wonder.

"Did you get it yet, Matt?"

"I couldn't miss it. God, I am such an idiot."

Michelle giggled. "Yeah, but most guys are. Um, is that *all* you read?"

"No." I felt her stiffen again. "How long have you been in love with me?"

"A couple of years. I-" Her voice caught, and she ducked her head, unwilling to meet my gaze.

"Amateur."

Michelle raised her head and met my eyes with hers. "What does *that* mean?"

"I've been in love with you since the sixth grade."

"You're making that up."

"Oh yeah? Now you read *me*." I resumed kissing her.

Much later, Michelle laid her head on my shoulder, her breath tickling my neck.

"Okay, Matt, I believe you."

"I guess this means you're not going to file a psychic incident report and collect the big reward Psi Corps offers for discovering a rogue psychic?"

"Don't tell me you were worried about that."

"Nah. Not even *before* that kiss. You've never been that kind of girl."

"You figured that out, did you?"

"All by myself."

Michelle ruffled my hair. "Good. Because now I need you to tell me everything you can about your psychic abilities."

"Sure, but do I have to do that now?"

"Absolutely. I can't make plans if I don't know what I'm dealing with."

"Plans for what, Michelle?"

"Rescuing your parents, of course."

THE SEARCH BEGINS

Now it was my turn to pull back and catch Michelle's eyes. I didn't need psychic abilities to read her determination.

"There's nothing I would rather do right now than fly off in this spaceship and search for my parents. But an hour ago, I told Jonas I would put it off for at least seven years. I can't risk people's lives over that. Not your father's. Not yours." I kissed Michelle gently. "Especially not yours."

"That's very gallant, Matt. Stupid, but gallant."

"Uh, what?"

"I've had lots of training dealing with threats, Matt. *Real* training, not the pulled-punches kind of stuff most people get. Do you think Daddy would have added me to your bodyguard detail if I couldn't hack it?"

Jonas had fired more than one bodyguard for inattention on duty, poor decision-making, or poor combat techniques. The man would never risk Michelle or me if he didn't know his daughter was up to the task. I shook my head.

"I can't match strength with a man my own size, much less one a lot larger than me, but I *do* know how to beat them. I fight to win and that means I fight dirty." Michelle's expression flowed from intense to innocent, from simple to sultry. Then she pulled her shoulders back, thrusting her breasts out in the way guys always notice. "And I use every single weapon at my disposal to distract my opponents and make them underestimate me.

"Daddy started training me to handle myself long before he ever started working for your father. You might have to save my ass someday, but it will be because of something we've gotten into *together*. I'm not some fairy tale princess, so don't start treating me like one."

"As you command, Your Highness."

"Good. Don't forget that."

"I won't—but it doesn't change what I told Jonas. He's off arranging for me to assign control of my inheritance to my uncle. You understand my motivations, now, but no one else does."

"And you can't risk telling anyone for fear they'll report you to Psi Corps. That would be the perfect way for your enemies to get rid of you, too. You disappear into the Corps and their lives return to normal." Michelle sat back, looking thoughtful. "If you told Daddy, he would understand what drives you, but he would still try to stop you from acting on it."

"And that puts me right back where we were an hour ago, except you know my secret. I need money to fund a full-scale search but, this time tomorrow, I won't control very much of my own money."

"Maybe... There's something niggling in the back of my mind, Matt." Michelle cocked her head. "Tell me more about your psychic ability."

"There's nothing to tell that you haven't already seen. I've never felt emotions as strongly as I did earlier tonight." I ran my hands through her hair. "Of course, I've never been touched quite so intimately, before."

"No, not that ability. You also said you can *feel* your parents wherever they are."

"Yeah. They have a presence in my mind. Aunt Tess is there, too, though her presence is weaker and I can only pick her up when she's nearby. It's the same with my grandparents. I can't pick up my cousins unless I'm in the same room with them and concentrate really hard."

Michelle bit her lower lip, something she did when puzzling through a problem.

"Matt, I want to try something. Please just go along with me, don't think, just do what comes naturally."

"I'll try."

"No, don't try. Feel. 'Trying' could screw this up."

Michelle cut off any reply by kissing me. As before, it was a long, sensuous kiss straight from my fantasies. Even if I'd wanted to think or try, I couldn't have. Conscious thought fled, and I reveled in the feelings of the moment. Michelle's kisses roamed all over my face as her fingers combed through my hair. She even nibbled playfully on my ear.

"Point to your parents."

Michelle's whisper didn't register in my conscious mind. I didn't even realize she'd spoken until my arm shot up and out. Michelle clapped her hands together and shrieked with joy.

"It worked!"

My arm still pointing off into space, I said, "Obviously, I'm missing something here. What worked?"

"You're pointing toward your parents."

"Yeah, and probably a trillion other beings. And it's not like a pointing arm is a precision instrument. Even a tiny discrepancy in direction becomes huge when you're measuring distance in light years."

"I know all that, Matt. We took the same classes, remember? And I was always better at geometry than you were. We'll need more measurements than this one, but if we can get three or four more, we can triangulate on a star chart and narrow the search down to one or two star systems."

"And *then* I could use my ability to guide us to my parents." It was my turn to pull Michelle into a deep kiss. "You are the smartest, most beautiful, most wonderful, most amazing girl ever. God, I love you!"

"I love you too," Michelle laughed. "And, as much fun as it is making out with you, hadn't we better get started making preparations for the search?"

"Why? Once we tell people-" Comprehension dawned on me. "We can't tell anyone because then we'd have to explain how I was guiding the search."

Michelle nodded. "There's one more reason we need to keep this a secret. Whoever is trying to stop you from liquidating your inheritance might be the person behind your parents' disappearance."

That thought hadn't occurred to me.

"You're saying I'm on my own."

"No, Matt, I'm saying *we* are on *our* own. And we need to get started before you sign any legal papers."

"What about Jonas? He'll be worried sick about us."

"Daddy and I have ways of leaving messages for each other. He won't understand why I'm doing this and he'll worry, but at least he'll know what we're doing."

"Money is going to be tight. Spaceships are expensive to run and I only have access to my trust fund dividends right now."

"I've got some money, too. Daddy made sure I banked most of my bodyguard salary. And if the money runs out, we'll just have to find some way to get more."

The next five hours passed in a blur of activity. I fueled the ship, restocked provisions, and filed a flight plan for a simple run around the solar system. We wouldn't follow it for long but the plan would get us off the planet. When accompanied by bodyguards, I took similar flights all the time. I had Michelle guarding me, so Jonas shouldn't think twice about it when space control informed him of the filing. At the last moment, Michelle and I transferred all the money in our bank accounts onto a few credit sticks.

Then it was time to go. I lifted off, soaring through the brightening morning sky and into space. At long last, the search for my parents was on.

An hour into our flight, Michelle took time to compose a message for Jonas.

"Daddy setup a bunch of different message drops so I can send and receive messages without using a comm, since those are so easy to intercept."

"Don't you use encrypted comms? I mean, even I have one of them to use for sensitive calls."

"Of course we have encrypted comms, Matt, but how many girls use an encrypted comm to call their father?"

"I'm guessing not a lot?"

Michelle shook her head. "You're pretty clueless when it comes to girls, aren't you?"

"In my own defense, I have had my eye on one girl in particular for about as long as I've been interested in girls in general."

"Oh, really? What do you call that little thing you had with Jayna two years ago?"

"An attempt to make you jealous and get you to pay attention to me."

Michelle stopped composing and looked up from her pad. "Seriously?"

"Yes."

"Well, it worked. I was thrilled when she broke up with you after two weeks."

I barked a humorless laugh. "Jayna didn't break up with me. She just picked a different target."

"I'm sure you're going to explain what you mean by that."

"Jayna isn't as good at cloaking her emotions as you, Michelle. A week into our relationship, she held my hand as we walked to a class. While she smiled and giggled and chattered about how wonderful I was, her real emotion was greed tinged with desperation. She wasn't interested in *me* at all. My *money* was a different matter entirely."

Michelle nodded slowly. "If she could make you fall in love with her and then stick with you long enough to get married, she'd be rich beyond her wildest dreams. But I know Jayna and that kind of delayed gratification, much less long term planning, just isn't in her nature."

"And it wasn't her plan then, either. I did a little research that evening and found out her father was nearly bankrupt and decided to use his best remaining asset to restore the family fortune. Actually, Jonas is the one who found out that last part and the rest of the plan. I just told him I'd caught Jayna looking at me oddly and he took it from there."

"Daddy never told me about that. What was Jayna's plan?"

"To get pregnant and use the baby to extort a big payday from my family. Allegations of date rape were a possibility, along with child support payments and anything else Jayna's family lawyers could come up with."

"God, it must have hurt to be seen as nothing more than a big wallet."

I sighed. "It did, though I took perverse pleasure in appearing blind to Jayna's attempts to seduce me."

"So that's why Jayna started the rumors that you were gay."

Michelle's words triggered a connection. "Were you the one who started the counter rumor?"

"That a couple of the maids in your house were tutoring you in the ways of love? Absolutely."

"Thanks, though I felt bad for the maids' reputations when I first heard the rumor. When I apologized to them about the rumors, they just laughed and told me not to worry about it."

"Oh, they already knew, Matt. Daddy asked their permission before I started the rumor. Jayna treated them like she did everyone else—with condescension—so they were happy to help."

"Why didn't you ever tell me how you felt? Just a few hours ago, Jonas said it would be useful for you to be my girlfriend, that you'd have an excuse to be with me wherever I went. Why not do that throughout school?"

"Daddy did ask me to do that after the Jayna incident. Keep the other girls at bay and all that."

"Why didn't you go along with it? You know it would have worked."

"It would have—right up until you found out I was one of your bodyguards. You'd have assumed it was just business for me and I'd have lost you forever."

"No I wouldn't. Not after we kissed. I'd have read your true emotions."

"Yeah, well, I didn't know you were psychic, did I?"

"Oh. Good point."

"Now, let me finish this note to Daddy. We're going to have to break from the flight plan soon and I want the message in place when we do."

Michelle let me read the note before she sent it.

Dear Daddy, My new boyfriend asked me to come along on a trip. Remember that gift he wanted to go looking for? I'm going to help him find it. I'll see you when we get back. Hugs to Mom and don't worry.

"Nice work, Michelle. This won't make sense to anyone who wasn't part of our conversation last night."

"There's a bit more to it than that. The last sentence is code asking him to cover for your absence."

"Just mine? What about you?"

"I'm not supposed to inherit billions of credits late this afternoon. No one is going to think twice if I'm out of sight for a while."

Ten minutes later, I broke from my flight plan and flew for the nearest wormhole.

"Daddy's response just arrived, but keep your mind on piloting. We can discuss it once we've entered the wormhole."

Then the wormhole opened before us and the solar system I called home vanished.

Michelle gasped at the sudden transition from normal space to whatever it was that formed the inside of a wormhole. One second, the view port showed deep blackness interspersed with tiny sparks of light. The next second, gray nothingness cloaked our ship.

"That's just creepy, Matt. It's like we're encased in the thickest fog ever seen. God only knows what strange and monstrous things lurk just beyond our sight."

She shuddered. Ever the caring young man, I put an arm around Michelle and pulled her close.

"It's just the inside of a wormhole. You get used to it after a while."

"Have you never wondered if anything else was inside the wormhole with you? Wondered if maybe something within the wormhole was behind ship disappearances?"

"I don't know. Maybe I did when I was little. If so, I was too young to remember it." I shrugged. "I think there would be more wormhole disappearances if something living inside the wormhole was behind them."

Michelle gave a second shudder. "Maybe it doesn't get hungry very often..."

Now the gray nothingness was starting to creep me out, too. It was time to change the subject.

"So, what did Jonas' message say?"

"What?" Michelle brought her gaze around to face me and it seemed some tension went out of her. I decided it would be best to keep her attention away from the view port and her attention off of undiscovered and, I hoped, non-existent wormhole creatures.

"The reply from your father. What did it say?"

"Oh, right. Hang on."

Michelle bent over her pad for a few seconds before handing it to me.

Dear Daughter, I am unsettled over this development. I would like to know more about this beau before you take such a long trip. Stay in touch and don't forget to be successful.

"Most of that makes sense, I guess. But what's that bit about being successful? Is that another code phrase?"

Michelle looked away. "It sort of is, but that's Daddy-speak rather than codewords for work."

"What does it mean?"

"Mom and Daddy have drilled certain ideas into me over the years. The path to success was one they harped on over and over." Michelle paused for a few seconds. When she resumed speaking, it was obvious she was reciting something. "To be successful, finish school before you get married and get married before you have children."

There was lots of data backing up that simple advice, so I nodded. "Yeah, my aunt and uncle have told me basically the same thing. So what?"

"I think Daddy figured out how I feel about you watching the way I reacted to you last night."

"Okay. What's that got to do with—? Oh! Um, I see."

"Yep, this is Daddy's subtle way of telling me not to get pregnant. Remind me to kick him in the shin when we get back."

"So, are there any other messages hidden inside his message?"

"Yes, there's an actual code phrase in there, as well. The bit about staying in touch means he's going to claim you've been kidnapped."

"Kidnapped? I guess it will explain what happened to us-"

"To you. No one will wonder about me."

"*I* would have wondered about you."

"And you're very sweet, Matt, but no one else will. But 'keep in touch' actually means I have to find a way to send an untraceable ransom note."

"Have you got a way to do that or will you need my help?"

"You know how to send untraceable messages?"

"Your father kind of forced me to learn."

Michelle bit her lip, the sign that she was puzzling through something. "I guess I can see why Daddy *might* want you to know how to do that..."

She looked annoyed when I laughed. "I'm sorry to laugh, Michelle. But Jonas didn't teach me how to do that. I had to figure it out for myself—along with all the other things I had to learn so I could get away from him and the other bodyguards every now and then. You have no idea how much fun it was to send untraceable messages to Jonas telling him I wasn't in my room."

"And I'm sure Daddy just *loved* getting those messages from you. You know, he never came out and said it, but I know your ingenuity impressed him. I bet you never thought you'd get to use that ingenuity to send your own ransom note."

Michelle spent the rest of the wormhole jump composing a ransom note.

I spent the jump changing the ship's registration beacon. Switching out the beacon isn't difficult, but reprogramming one is a real bear of a job. I paid a smuggler to teach me how to do it, just in case I had to sneak off to rescue my parents. Exactly what I was doing now, in other words.

"What do you think we ought to call the ship?" I asked.

"I don't know. What was its old name?"

"Dad and I never got around to naming it. It was always just the spaceship. We wouldn't be on this trip if it wasn't for you, so I think we should name if after you."

"The *Michelle*? Even if no one knows I'm gone, that's not obscure enough for my tastes."

"Then how about the *Blonde Bombshell?*"

The look Michelle gave me spoke volumes.

"I guess that means the *Blonde Beauty* is out, too?"

"Yes, as is the *Curvy Cutie*, the *Blue-Eyed Blonde*, and any other name based on my body parts."

"Well, what do you suggest we name the ship?"

Michelle pondered for a moment before a smile brightened her face.

"How about naming it after both of us while still keeping it kind of obscure?"

"Okay. What did you have in mind?"

"Let's call it the *M&M*."

An hour later, my spaceship finally had a name.

ROCKVILLE STATION

Ten days, four wormhole jumps, and four of what Michelle had taken to calling 'parental pointings' later, I could feel my nerves unraveling. This was supposed to be *so* simple —we would hop around our part of the galaxy, I'd point two or three times, and we'd narrow our search down to one or two star systems. Life had not cooperated.

It turns out that arms not only are not precision directional instruments, they're downright horrible ones. Four pointings into our search and we still had twenty-three possible star systems to consider. Yeah, we had eliminated billions of other stars, but this was going a lot slower than I had expected.

"Don't beat yourself up over this, Matt. We're making progress, even if it's not as fast as you'd like." Michelle kneaded my shoulders as I maneuvered the *M&M* to dock with an out-of-the-way station in an out-of-the-way star system. "Your shoulders are as hard as the ore they mine in this system."

The comm crackled. "Starship *M&M*, we have you in the station tractor beam. Stop all engines and let us bring you in."

My hands flew over the control panel. "Roger that, Rockville Station. All engines stopped."

"You're currently fourth in line for refueling, *M&M*. Figure on a wait of four T hours. We'll comm you when we're ready for you." An amused tone entered the voice crackling from the comm. "Why not stretch your legs a bit and see the sight?"

"Sight, singular?" I asked.

"You're on the ass end of nowhere, boyo. We're lucky we've got *one* sight. Every bar on the station has a view of it, but the best one is in a joint called Ore Sons."

"Let me guess, Orson is your cousin." Anyone who ever watched vids knew how this sort of thing worked.

"First, it's Ore. Sons. As in sons of the ore. I'd say it's a miner's bar, but all of them are miner's bars around here. Second, I don't have a cousin named Orson."

"Sorry, Rockville Control. I guess I watched too many vids growing up." Maybe the guy was part owner of the joint. Still, it couldn't hurt to stay on the good side of the local authorities. "Do they serve food at Ore Sons? Shipboard rations get old real fast."

A laugh sounded from the comm. "Ain't that the truth of it? They sling the best burgers in the system."

With a soft clang, we completed docking with the station.

"You've convinced me, Control. I'll tell 'em you sent me."

"Mighty kind of you, *M&M*. Please enjoy your stay on lovely Rockville Station."

I flipped the comm off and leaned back. Michelle's hands kept working on my shoulders. It felt really good, but I was too restless to truly enjoy it.

Standing, I wrapped an arm around Michelle's waist. "How about I treat my best girl to a burger and fries?"

"Gee, Matt, you take me to all the best places." In contrast to her sarcastic tone, Michelle's eyes lit up. "You know, I've never been on a space station before. This is kind of exciting."

I took Michelle's hand and led her toward the hatch. "Have you ever been to a shopping mall?"

"Of course." Her tone implied an accompanying eye roll.

"The only difference between a shopping mall and a space station is what's outside of it." After we buckled blasters to our hips, I cycled the airlock, and we stepped out of the ship for the first time in a week and a half. "And space station air has a stronger recycled smell to it than spaceship air."

Walking through the docks, I discovered another difference between shopping malls and backwater space stations. Shopping malls are teeming with pretty girls. Backwater space stations, not so much. Every male eye tracked Michelle, some of the men going so far as to stop working or walking and stare openly at her. Busy looking at everything, a big smile plastered on her face, Michelle didn't notice the stares.

"I think we should go back to the ship, Michelle." My gaze darted all around, looking for any possible threat from the men around us.

"Why? Because all the men are staring at me?"

"You noticed?"

"I'm a trained bodyguard, Matt. Of course I noticed." Her sweeping gaze met mine for a second. "If I fooled you, then I fooled them, too."

"So you see why we should go back to the ship?"

The memory of my run in with the gang on the maglev train was still fresh in my mind. Facing a repeat of that experience, this time with Michelle beside me, had no appeal to me.

"No way, buster. You promised me a burger and fries. Besides, none of these guys are going to do anything but look at me."

I tried staring down some of the more obvious oglers in the crowd. To a man, they ignored me.

"How can you tell they won't try something?"

"These guys all follow me with their eyes for a while, then they go back to their work. I'm just a distraction, a bit of fantasy to get them through their day. Real troublemakers would tail us, making rude comments in the hope you'd overreact and give them an excuse to start a fight." Her hand brushed the blaster on her hip. "Besides, we *are* prepared for trouble."

Men continued to stare, but Michelle's read on them was right. No one tailed us or even spoke to us during the five minute walk to Ore Sons, but I still breathed a sigh of relief when we entered the bar.

Through a transparent wall, we had a fantastic view of the system's gas giant. It glowed orange with golden clouds swirling across the surface. I'd been told Saturn, back in Sol system, was the most beautiful planet in the Federation. If so, the planet before us must run a close second.

I felt Michelle stiffen beside me and dragged my attention away from Rockville Station's lone sight. Four young men rose from a table in a dark corner of the bar. I was immediately reminded of the gang on the maglev train.

"Hey, hey, hey, looky here, boys." The man spoke in a light-hearted sing-song, but he had a predator's eyes. "Someone brought us a pretty little present. Let's take her home and unwrap her."

Michelle sighed, real regret in her voice. "So much for the burger and fries."

The leader of the little gang swaggered out of the corner of the bar, his three buddies snickering and trailing him. You can find guys like him in every dark and dingy little corner of the Federation—and in just as many bright and prosperous corners. I didn't even have to speak with the guy to know he thought himself a supreme badass, a man who men feared and women wanted.

I hated him on sight.

The barkeep sighed. "I don't want no trouble in here, Paco. Take it out into the corridor."

"Ain't gonna be no trouble, Tom. Leastwise, not if this boy knows what's good for him."

That exchange answered another question. Paco had more than attitude; he wielded some actual power in the station. He was too young and too cocksure to have earned his power. That meant he got it by proxy, probably through his father.

"Aw, isn't he cute, Matt?" Michelle's pose looked casual, but her balance was evenly distributed and her right hand hung just below the handle of her blaster. "Do you want me to drop him and his little friends?"

That brought Paco and pals up short. It wasn't what Michelle said, so much as how she had said it. Her voice held absolute conviction that she would have no trouble handling all four of them. Now it was my turn.

"No, not after we came all this way to speak to Paco." I smiled at him. "At least, not yet."

Paco's face screwed up as he tried to figure out why the scene wasn't going as expected.

"What do you mean, you came here to speak to me?"

"Not you exactly, Paco. But you're on the list. I wasn't going to start until after I'd eaten, but with you turning up right here and all..." I walked over Paco and thrust out my hand. "I'm pleased to meet you."

Paco's eyes darted between my outstretched hand, my smile, and Michelle, confusion written all over his face.

One of the three pals got tired of waiting for something to happen. "Hey, Paco, we gonna mess the guy up and take the girl or what?"

I shook my head in disappointment. "A true leader keeps his lackeys in line and under his control."

"Who you callin' a lackey, boy?"

Ignoring the blustering follower, I reached out and took Paco's right hand in mine. "In civilized society, when a man offers you his hand, you shake it."

To emphasize my words, I added my left hand to the grip and slowly shook Paco's hand up and down. This was what I had been aiming for all along. As expected, Paco had no control over his emotions. Confident of his high standing within Rockville Station society, he had never felt the need to conceal his feelings from anyone.

Paco's emotions were laid bare for me to read. With a few carefully chosen words, I could also manipulate them.

Paco's lackey spoke up again. "Hey, Paco, you gonna let him talk like that 'bout us?"

I felt confusion giving way to consideration in Paco's mind. This was no time for me to let him start thinking about things.

"Michelle, I find it difficult to think with the lackey's yammering. If you would?"

The lackey danced forward, raising a fist. "If she would, what, boy?"

A blaster report echoed through the bar, followed by a thump as the lackey fell to the floor.

Terror surged in Paco's mind, driving away all attempts at rational thought. I had been aiming for fear and confusion, not terror.

"Don't worry, Paco, he'll be fine." I turned my head in Michelle's direction. "You did have the blaster set to stun, didn't you?"

"Of course." Michelle turned a serious look on Paco. "Do you have any idea how much paperwork is involved if I kill someone in the line of duty?"

Wide-eyed, Paco could only shake his head.

Michelle flashed a sweet smile. "There are so many forms, I sometimes wish I was the auditor instead of the arresting officer."

I could have kissed Michelle right then. I'd been looking for the right words to spark emotions in Paco and she had gone right to them.

"A-auditor?"

Paco's confusion was swept away, leaving only fear. Fear for his position on the station and, much less powerful, fear for his father.

"Oh, didn't I mention my position, Paco? I am sorry for the oversight."

"Um, I, uh, gotta go, now."

"Of course. You probably want to take your friend to a doctor, just as a precaution. You never know who's going to have an allergic reaction to stun bolts."

"Right. Yeah. That." Paco motioned to his two remaining lackeys, who picked up the one on the floor.

"Remember, my visit is a surprise. Don't say a word to your father." I checked my chrono. "I want to eat and get settled into our rooms before going to your father's office. Why don't you meet me there in, say, five hours?"

"You got it, sir." Paco and his friends walked wide around Michelle and disappeared into the main corridor.

Michelle and I watched them go, then took seats at the bar.

"We don't get no auditors out here," the barkeep said. "You know Paco's gonna run right to his daddy."

"Yep. I'm counting on it." I saw no reason to drop the part. You never knew who was listening. "We'll each have a cheeseburger and fries."

The man yelled the order over his shoulder and got an answering yell from the kitchen.

"You ain't worried 'bout them hiding all their books and stuff while you sit here eating?"

I pulled out my pad and started flipping through menus. "Who said I was just eating?"

When the barkeep left to help another customer, Michelle leaned in close.

"You aren't actually planning to try to do an audit, are you?"

"Are you kidding? I wouldn't have the foggiest idea what to look for." I turned to her and kissed the end of her nose. "That whole auditor and arresting officer bit was brilliant, by the way."

"Thank you. It seemed to fit the whole Man of Mystery spiel you were spinning." She leaned closer to see what I was doing on my pad. Her eyebrows rose in surprise. "Why are you using one of my father's message drops?"

"GenCo holds most of the ore contracts with Rockville Station. I looked it up before we jumped into the system."

"So?"

"I thought it might be a good idea to have a real auditor pay this place a visit."

Michelle buried her head in my shoulder and laughed.

A moment later, the barkeep dropped two plates in front of us. The guy in Rockville Control was right. The burger was delicious.

We spent the next several hours poking around the station. Rockville Control pinged me when they started refueling the ship. We were heading back to the *M&M* when the ambush came.

AMBUSH

Hand in hand, Michelle and I wandered back toward the docking bay. Other than our encounter with Paco and his pals, we'd had a good time on Rockville Station. There wasn't anything of any real interest on the station, but that was the point. We cuddled while looking at the spectacular view of the system's gas giant. We strolled down the main corridor, ducking into the odd shop just to see what was what. We bought a few trinkets from station crafters.

It was nothing special, and that's what made it special. We were just a couple out on a do-nothing date. No one gave us a second glance. Well, no one gave *me* a second glance. Michelle got a lot of second glances, but after our walk into the station through the docks, I decided it wouldn't bother me if it didn't bother Michelle. The day was so different than any other day I'd ever spent that I was disappointed when station control notified me that refueling was complete.

Nearing our docking bay, Michelle was the first to realize something was amiss. Holding hands, I felt her emotions shift from contented to concerned.

"Pretend like everything is fine," she whispered, smiling brightly at me.

"Okay." I looked around us as casually as possible. "But, I don't see anything to be worried about."

"*That* is what you should worry about. This place was full of dock workers when we came into the station. Now it's empty."

"Maybe the work shift is over?"

"It's only four in the afternoon, local time."

"It is?" I'd completely lost track of everything other than Michelle. "So, what do we do?"

"We can keep acting casual and draw out Paco and his gang or we can make a run for it."

I opened my mouth to ask why she thought it was Paco and then shut it again. I'd embarrassed Paco in front of his followers. Guys like him always felt like they had to get even for things like that.

We were about midway through one of the docking compartments, one about a quarter of a kilometer long. I figured Paco's father owned everything in the compartment and employed everyone who worked here, giving Paco the authority he needed to clear the area. If we could just get to the next compartment, we'd probably be safe.

"You're the bodyguard. What do you think we should do?"

"Run. *Now!*"

Shouts erupted as soon as we broke into a sprint. A couple of blaster bolts sizzled past, well wide of the mark. Both shots scorched the deck where they hit.

"They're shooting to kill, Matt!"

Drawing her own blaster, Michelle thumbed off the stun setting. I did the same.

Behind us, we heard feet pounding on the deck. To the side, we saw young men pop up from behind crates and take aim at us.

Michelle snapped off three quick shots to the right, and I did the same to the left. My shots went wild, but Michelle blasted apart a crate one guy hid behind. He screamed as splinters flayed him.

I half turned and fired at the four or five guys behind us. Again,

I didn't hit anyone, but they scattered, diving behind crates or dropping to the deck.

"Nice shooting, honey." Michelle fired a few shots at the guys on the right, again blasting apart a crate.

"I was trained by the best."

I fired shots to the left, again. One shot burned the deck next to one of Paco's shooters. He yelped and ducked out of sight.

"Matt, look out!"

Michelle shoved me hard to the left. A blaster bolt seared the air where I'd been standing. Thrown off balance, I stumbled and fell. All sorts of training took over at that point, from gymnastics to martial arts. I tucked into a roll as I heard another bolt hit the deck somewhere behind me.

"You made me miss my shot, bitch."

Paco's voice sounded different than he had in the bar. It was wilder, even less in control than he'd been a few hours ago.

"Your boyfriend made me look stupid in front of my father."

I heard him take another shot and felt my blood run cold. The weapon's report was deeper, the sound of the bolt striking the deck louder. Without looking up, I knew Paco had gotten his hands on a blaster rifle. A person might survive shots from a pistol, but a rifle could blow away half a person's body with any hit.

"I was going to kill him," Paco raved on, "and save you for some fun. I'd have let you go eventually, but then you had to go and shove him away from my shot."

I came out of my roll and up onto one knee.

To my right, Michelle was on the deck, rolling away from Paco's shots. She was using all her training to good effect, but had too far to go to reach any kind of cover. Paco's next shot seared the deck centimeters from her head.

"So I'm going to kill you in front of your boyfriend and then I'll throw him out an airlock."

I raised my blaster in a two-handed grip, just like Jonas had taught me. At the same time, Paco took aim for another shot at Michelle.

"Hey, Paco!"

My shout distracted him just for a second, delaying his next shot at Michelle. I pulled the trigger, pulled it again, and then pulled it a third time. The first shot hit Paco in the shoulder. The next two hit him right in the middle of the chest.

Paco's eyes went wide, a puzzled look crossing his face. Then the light went out of Paco's eyes and his body fell to the deck.

I watched Paco fall backward. Saw his body bounce slightly as it hit the deck. Watched a wisp of smoke spiral up from Paco's chest. Heard nothing beyond the roaring of my blood and the pounding of my heart.

Movement came from my right and an angel, with deep blue eyes and a halo of golden hair, slid between me and Paco. She grabbed my shoulder and shouted at me, but I couldn't understand what she was saying. Though she blocked my view of Paco, I still saw him with my mind's eye. Saw the spiraling wisp of smoke thicken and the hole in Paco's chest burning brighter, consuming Paco in an ever-widening circle.

Sharp pain exploded from my left cheek, and then from my right cheek. I blinked and the angel's face swam into focus.

"I killed him, Michelle."

"I know, Matt, and I'll help you deal with it. But right now we've got to get out of here."

Michelle leaned to the side, gripping her blaster with both hands, and snapped off five shots in quick succession.

"Paco's boys are getting over their shock, Matt. We're going to die here if you can't put Paco out of your mind until we're safe."

My memory replayed the blaster bolts burning a hole in the chest, but this time it was Michelle's chest. That brought me out of it.

Spinning on my knees, I added my blaster fire to Michelle's. Paco's gang scattered from our combined fire, still skittish after seeing their leader killed.

Michelle jumped to her feet, pulling me up with her. "Let's go!"

We dashed toward the door out of this compartment, the door

that led to safety. As we sprinted past Paco, Michelle bent over and scooped up Paco's blaster rifle. A bright flash splattered against the wall near the door, followed by another one.

Michelle spun about and fired the blaster rifle from the hip. "Keep running. Get the door open."

The deep report of the rifle echoed again and again as Michelle laid down covering fire for me. I smacked the control for the door and it began grinding open.

"Michelle! Come on."

Already backpedaling in my direction, Michelle turned and ran. I dashed through and found the controls on the other side. A bolt scorched the deck just inside the door as Michelle slipped through the widening opening. I slapped the controls, and the door reversed itself, grinding shut again.

"The ship?" I asked as we ran from the doors.

"Yes." Michelle gasped.

All around us, dockworkers stared. Then another bolt flew through the closing door. It didn't hit anyone, but it startled the workers into action. They dove behind crates and ran clear of our path.

I heard the door's mechanism give a clunk as it reversed yet again. Blaster shots echoed in this new compartment and the air around us was filled with little bolts of lightning. Then we ran out of the compartment and into the docking bay. The airlock to the *M&M* was just meters away.

We ran past a surprised station official waving a datapad in my direction.

"Hey, you need to approve the charges."

Michelle and I slid through the outer airlock.

"I trust you. Keep my deposit. And I'd run if I were you."

We slammed the outer hatch in his face. I spun the locking wheel while Michelle opened the inner hatch.

"Take the controls and get us moving, Matt. I'll seal the hatches."

"On it!"

I slid into the pilot seat of the ship and keyed the emergency startup sequence. It skipped a few safety protocols and wasted energy, but we didn't have five minutes to go through the normal sequence. Michelle slipped into the copilot chair as the startup completed.

"Can you break free of the docking clamps and the tractor beam?" Her brow was furrowed in concern.

"Don't believe everything you see in the vids, Michelle. Military tractor beams are the only ones strong enough to stop a ship. The magnetic docking clamps aren't strong enough to hold us, either."

Muffled banging began on the station hatch. Too late to stop us, Paco's boys had caught up.

I shoved the maneuvering thrusters to full throttle. The ship bucked a bit as it broke free of the magnetic clamps and shook again as it pulled out of the tractor beam.

Rockville Station didn't attract much starship traffic, but it had a lot of in-system mining ships coming and going at all times. Much as I wanted to just punch the throttle and blast toward the wormhole on a column of fusion-powered flame, I couldn't. My hands flew over the ship's controls, weaving in and out of the local ships as fast as I could manage.

"*M&M*, this is Rockville Control. You are not cleared for departure and are ordered to return to the station."

Michelle took the comm. "No can do, Rockville Control. We've got a pressing appointment somewhere else."

A new voice replaced the controller. "This is Station Security Chief Tucker. You *will* return to this station for questioning concerning the death of a station citizen."

"I'm sorry, Chief, but I rather doubt we'll get a fair hearing."

"We're not as backward as you think, miss. We've got a circuit-riding Psi Corps team. Their telepath will determine guilt and innocence."

"Good. When the telepath questions Paco's gang, you'll get all the evidence you need to clear us. So, you see there's no reason for us to stick around."

I was almost clear of the local traffic. From there, it was a five minute flight to the wormhole—less at the speed I'd be flying.

A new voice joined the comm conversation. The voice was harsh, and I found myself taking an immediate dislike to its unseen owner.

"You can back off, Chief. Me and my boys are gonna take care of these killers."

"Hector, tell your boys to leave that ship alone and dock at the station. You can't take justice into your own hands."

"They killed my boy, Chief. I can do anything I damn well want."

A hulking asteroid mining ship, bristling with mining lasers, broke free of the station traffic, blocking our path to the wormhole!

A SURPRISE IN THE DEBRIS FIELD

Dozens of one man mining sleds buzzed around the huge asteroid mining ship, speeding into a formation spread across dozens of kilometers. Within seconds the sleds formed a cone with the mining ship at its center.

"What are they doing?" Michelle asked.

"It's a fighting formation miners developed to battle against pirates."

I ordered the nav computer to calculate the fastest course around the formation. It might turn up something I couldn't see, but I doubted it. These miners knew their stuff. As long as they held the cone together, they could block the *M&M* from ever reaching the wormhole.

"Can you get around them, Matt?" Her voice remained calm as if she was simply checking off items on a list.

The nav computer beeped, confirming my observation.

"Not unless they do something foolish, no."

Rockville Control came back on the comm. "Hector, tell your ships to come on into the docking bay. Your guys have already worked a full shift and have got to be exhausted. You don't want them doing something stupid just because they're too tired to think straight."

That explained how the mining ship and the sleds mobilized so quickly. They were already outside, waiting for a chance to dock, when we pulled out.

"As long as one of my boys blasts that ship, I don't care what they do. And I'll give a big bonus to every single one of them when those murderers are breathing vacuum."

Michelle decided to rejoin the conversation. "It was self-defense, not murder. Paco and about a dozen of his gang ambushed us on our way back to our ship."

"If that's true, little girl, why aren't you dead instead of my son?"

"Because we're better than he was. But that's no surprise, Hector. After all, Paco only got away with all his bullying because he was riding on your coattails."

Hector roared in anger. Chief Tucker wasn't real happy with Michelle, either.

"Young lady, you are *not* helping matters and I will thank you to keep your mouth shut while I talk to Hector."

"I'll tell you what, Chief, why don't you tell me about all your run-ins with Paco? Why don't you tell me about all the stuff he got away with because his daddy was the richest man on the station?"

I spared a glance at Michelle and whispered, "What are you doing?"

She flicked the mic off. "I'm getting Hector to make a mistake."

"Like what, blasting us out of space?"

"Like ordering his men to chase after us." Michelle tapped something on the nav display. "Mentioning that, fly toward this debris field. The miners will think we're trying to hide from them in there."

"What will that do for us?"

"Hector's ships have been out all day. How much fuel do you think they have left? If we can run them dry, we'll be clear to make a run for the wormhole."

"That's brilliant, Michelle."

I plotted a course toward the debris field and engaged the main thrusters.

"I know, just make sure you don't lose them. Now concentrate on flying this thing and leave the talking to me."

Michelle flipped her mic on again. "Chief, I'm still waiting for you to tell me what a fine, upstanding young man Paco was and how everyone on the station just loved him to pieces. I went to school with at least a dozen spoiled little rich boys just like Paco. Tell me I'm wrong, Chief."

"Girl, are you trying to get yourself killed?" Chief Tucker sounded a bit frazzled, all of a sudden.

"Well, Chief, I got good news for the girl. She's gonna get what she wants." Hector's voice dripped with menace. "Boys, I promised you a bonus if you blasted that ship. The bonus is a year's pay for everyone involved. Now go get 'em."

The cone of mining ships surged after us. The formation fractured a bit, but nothing you wouldn't expect with so many ships involved. The Federation Navy could hold a tighter formation, but I doubt many other civilian groups could have matched the miners.

The comm filled with whoops and threats from the pursuing mining ships. Chief Tucker tried talking them down, but the miners drowned him out every time he spoke. The Chief kept at it for a good thirty minutes before giving up. As best I could tell, Hector signed off once his ships were on our tail.

"*M&M*, this is Chief Tucker. If you manage to survive this, I still need you to surrender yourself to me."

"Seriously, Chief?" Michelle's voice held true incredulity. "After this demonstration from Paco's father, you really think we'd be safe anywhere on that station?"

The Chief sighed. "No, I don't. I had to say that for the record. Off the record, I'll get to the bottom of this and clear your names. Posthumously, if necessary."

"Thanks in advance for clearing us. But we don't plan on dying today."

If Chief Tucker replied, catcalls from the pursuing miners drowned him out.

Michelle flipped off the comm. "How long until we reach the debris field?"

"About another hour at this speed. I could shave fifteen minutes off of that at full power, but the miners couldn't keep up."

"Then steady as she goes, Captain Matt." Michelle took my hand. "Are you doing okay?"

I sighed. "I don't know. I'm fine as long as I'm active, but as soon as my mind has time to wander, it heads straight for the memory of me burning a hole in Paco's chest."

Michelle nodded and kissed my hand. "Let me know if there's anything I can do."

"How about a sandwich? That burger was hours ago. I know I shouldn't be hungry after everything, but my stomach hasn't gotten the message."

The next hour crawled past in slow motion. We ate. Michelle held my hand. I talked about everything except Paco. Finally, we approached the debris field.

"Um, Matt, are you going to fly through the field?"

"I thought that was the idea, Michelle? We use it to hide from the miners, letting them waste fuel looking for us."

"And get pulverized by asteroids? No thanks."

"There's nothing that big in there. This is the stuff left after the miners have broken up asteroids and removed the ore. The first mining operation in the system was probably here. It can dent the ship and scratch the paint, but that's about it."

I winced at every knock of a rock bouncing off the hull, but I managed to keep those to a minimum by throttling down and maneuvering carefully.

"Keep an eye on the sensors, Michelle. The debris will block a lot, but if you get a reading on that big mining ship, that means it's closer than I want it to be."

Ten minutes later, she said, "I just got the big ship on sensors."

Bracing myself, I increased the throttle. Stuff banged off the hull every few seconds, but we pulled out of sensor range of the big miner again. Then, without warning, the banging of rocks on the hull stopped.

"What the hell?" I asked.

"We're in a big empty spot in the debris field, Matt. It's like someone cleared all the debris out of this area with a vacuum or something."

The reason behind the empty spot became clear when a wormhole opened before us!

The wormhole blazed on the sensors and pulled the *M&M* inexorably toward its yawning maw. Debris from the field banged against our hull as the wormhole sucked up everything around it.

"Where did a wormhole come from?" Michelle asked. "It's not on any of the charts."

"Worry about that later." I snatched the comm from Michelle's hand, drawing a startled look. Glancing at the scanners as I keyed on the mic, I saw the big ship was once again close enough to register on them. "Pursuing mining ships, break off *now*! There is an open and uncharted wormhole just ahead of you. I repeat, *break off pursuit now!*"

A puzzled expression crossed Michelle's face. "What-?"

The comm crackled with static induced by the debris field. "Nice try, boyo. People been minin' this system for over a century. Ain't no way we got an uncharted wormhole."

"Scan the theta band, mining ship. I am deadly serious."

"You's doin' a good actin' job, kid. I give you that. Most people don't know minin' scanners don't go up to the theta band." The voice assumed false joviality. "Now, less'n you's gonna outbid our boss, we be comin' to get you."

"Yes! I will outbid your boss. Two years pay if you just *break off.*"

"Riiiiight. An' where's a kid like you gonna get that kind o' money?"

The building desperation in my voice convinced Michelle something was wrong. She leaned over and spoke into the mic.

"The kid is the heir to the Connaught fortune. He could buy Rockville Station with pocket change. He can pay you. Look, I don't know what this is all about, but there really is an open wormhole in front of us drawing our ship into it."

"Never mind, Michelle." The defeat in my voice was clear. "It's too late."

The mining ship and dozens of one man sleds burst out of the debris field and into the wormhole's field. As the cursing and screaming began, I switched off the comm. There were some things I just wasn't willing to listen to.

Michelle rubbed a hand up and down my arm. "I don't understand, Matt. What's the problem?"

"All those pursuing ships? They're designed for in-system work, not wormhole jumps." I looked into her still puzzled eyes. "None of those ships have inertial dampeners. When those ships enter the wormhole, they'll accelerate beyond light speed in an instant. Everyone on board will be blasted to atoms."

Her face paled. "Can't they change course or something?"

"Not this close to the wormhole. I don't know the physics behind wormholes, but you and I are the only ones who are going to still be alive thirty seconds from now."

Then we jumped and the gray fog of wormholes replaced the debris field.

During our first hour within the wormhole, Michelle listened to me and held me and talked to me and kissed me. I ranted about Paco and ranted even more about Paco's father and even railed at the miners for refusing to listen to me. I cried and then listened to Michelle. When she kissed me, I responded with a passion that surprised us both.

During our epic, hungry lip lock, Michelle's emotions shone bright and clear. I had her shirt unbuttoned before I knew what I was doing. Through a supreme force of will, I pulled myself back. I caught Michelle's hands as they tugged on my shirt.

"No. We need to stop."

In a breathless voice, Michelle said, "You're the empath, Matt. You know I want to do this."

"So do I. God knows, I want to." I leaned back and caught Michelle's eyes. "But not this way. Not for this reason. I want our first time to be loving and passionate and wonderful and not adrenaline-driven survivor sex."

Michelle leaned back, a small smile playing across her lips. "Isn't this what all guys fantasize about? A girl throwing herself at you after you heroically save her?"

I held her hand. "Yeah, we do. But it's always some fictitious beauty we've just met, not the girl we've loved for years."

Michelle pulled one knee up, rested her cheek against it, and gave me a coquettish smile. "Are you saying you don't have any fantasies about me?"

"Of course I do. But not that one." I took a deep breath and released it. "Please stop looking so damned irresistible. And button your shirt or I won't be able to concentrate on anything else."

We each took a few minutes to compose ourselves and straighten our clothes. Then Michelle fixed some coffee while I checked all the ship's systems to ensure everything was working properly.

Holding the warm mug, I sat opposite Michelle. "The hull took a beating near the end, but the systems are all fine." I patted the bulkhead next to me. "I expect she looks like an old beater of a ship, now, but she'll still get us where we want to go."

"And where do we want to go, Matt?"

"I guess that depends on what we find at the other end of this wormhole."

"How is it possible the wormhole isn't on any charts—especially since you figured the debris field was from the first mining outpost?"

"My best guess is some of the miners discovered it, but kept the discovery secret. It can't be a coincidence that a debris field surrounded the wormhole."

"But why keep it secret? Aren't wormholes good for business?" Michelle's eyebrows rose as an idea occurred to her. "Do you think those early miners set themselves up as pirates? It would be a lot easier to hit other miners and get away if the pirates had access to an unknown wormhole."

"The way our luck has been going today, you've likely hit on it." I sipped my coffee to give my thoughts a chance to sort themselves out. "We need to run dark after we exit the wormhole. If there are pirates on the other end, they're not going to take kindly to visitors."

We spent the rest of the wormhole jump planning for as many contingencies as possible. When the nav computer spoke, it startled both of us.

"Wormhole exit in one minute."

We shut down all extraneous systems, including all active sensors. Then we exited the wormhole. The mining vessels appeared around us, silent as the tombs they were. Michelle and I stared around us dumbly. She was the first to find her voice.

"I don't understand, Matt. Shouldn't there be a star somewhere nearby?"

The wormhole had dropped us in deep space, light years from the nearest star.

THE MESSENGER DRONE

W e floated along with the dead ships, staring out into a darkness whose perfection was broken only by bright pinpricks impossibly distant from us. The lack of planets or a nearby sun worked on our nerves.

As if afraid to speak out loud, Michelle whispered, "The wormhole we came through will open up from this end, won't it?"

"I've never heard of one that didn't open at both ends." Even to me, I sounded unsure. I tried again. "What I mean is of course it will."

"But have you ever heard of a wormhole ending in open space?" Michelle still whispered while staring out the viewport with wide eyes.

I pulled her into a hug. "I've never heard of a wormhole like this one, but remember that someone created that debris field to hide the wormhole. The only reason to do that is if they used it for some reason."

An unpleasant realization struck me. "And, when we don't return from the debris field, whoever knows about that wormhole is bound to come looking for us. We've got to hide."

"Hide where?" Michelle's voice was incredulous. "It's open space, Matt. There's nowhere *to* hide."

"Yeah, but we can set up a cover story for us, get clear of this funeral procession, and run dark."

Michelle shivered once, and I kicked myself for the funeral bit. But she rallied.

"What's your plan?"

"Blast a couple of the mining sleds into little pieces. If we're lucky, whoever comes looking will think the pieces are all that's left of the *M&M*. Meanwhile, we'll be floating somewhere a long way from here with all but our essential systems shutdown."

"And you're sure the systems will all start working again?" Michelle stopped whispering, but she still spoke in a small voice. "The ship took a hell of a beating before entering the wormhole."

"My father and I rebuilt every system in this ship. It'll take more than a few rocks to knock her systems out. But even if something is damaged, I can fix it."

Michelle nodded and, just like that, was herself again. "Okay, Cap'n, give me some targets and I'll blast 'em into a million pieces."

Moments later, she reduced a couple of sleds to fragments and then reduced the fragments to bits. By the time she was done, the *M&M's* sensors could no longer identify the source of the pieces.

"Wow that felt good. I never knew destroying stuff could be so therapeutic." She cocked her head in thought. "Is this why you guys hit walls and stuff when you're angry?"

"It is for me, anyway." I smiled at a memory. "My uncle insisted I repair the holes I punched in the walls at home. He said I had to learn that all actions had consequences."

"Did that make you stop punching the walls?"

"No. It turns out fixing the walls is kind of therapeutic, too. I ended up punching more walls just so I could fix them."

"That makes no sense, Matt."

"Really? Your father understood."

"Guys are weird."

"And yet you love us, anyway."

Coming up behind the pilot chair, Michelle wrapped her arms

around me and rubbed her cheek against mine. "Well, I love certain guys. But you're still weird."

"Oh, like you women are even remotely scrutable. Any guy who claims he understands women is either lying or certifiably insane."

Michelle's breath tickled my ear as she whispered, "Good. Our master plan is working."

I laughed and began maneuvering the *M&M* away from the mining ships. Michelle started to pull her arms back, but I caught them.

"I can pilot with your arms around me. Once we're clear of these ships, it's not like there's anything out here I can run into."

I punched a button and a dull *thunk* sounded from the bow of the ship.

"Did you just hit something, Matt? You said I wouldn't distract you."

"I just launched a directional relay. It can pick up comm broadcasts and beam them to us by laser. If more than one ship comes through, we should be able to pick up their conversations."

"Won't their sensors pick up the relay?"

"Probably not. All of these ships have power and their signatures should wash out the relay's power supply."

"Why would you have something like that onboard?"

"It's actually part of the required emergency supplies for a ship like this. It's supposed to be programmed to aim the laser at the nearest patrol station, but I reprogrammed this one to aim at the *M&M*."

That earned me a kiss on the cheek. "Aren't you a clever boy."

Michelle stayed there for a while longer before pulling back. "Are you hungry? I'm starving."

It had been hours since the sandwich which had been hours after the burger and fries. My stomach rumbled.

Michelle headed toward the galley. "I'll take that as a yes."

We ate while the ship pulled farther and farther from the dead flotilla. When we were about ten light minutes away, I brought the ship to a stop and began shutting down systems.

"Will we be able to see the wormhole open from here?" Michelle asked as she helped me power down the ship.

"If you're looking at exactly the right spot, it will look like one of those stars, flaring to life for a few seconds before fading away. The passive sensors will pick it up, though, along with whatever comes through. And the relay will pass along any comm traffic."

With the systems shut down, we settled in to wait. Two and a half hours later, sensors reported two ships exiting the wormhole and the comm burst to life. The relay worked perfectly.

"Where in the Nine Hells are we?"

I glanced at Michelle. "It sounds like Chief Tucker."

A new voice spoke from the comm. "How should I know? I found out about the wormhole at the same time you did."

In unison, Michelle and I said, "Paco's father."

"It was smack dab in the middle of your grandfather's claim, Hector. You expect me to believe he somehow managed to mine that patch of asteroids into little bits of rubble and never once figured out there was a wormhole in there?"

"I said *I* didn't know about the wormhole, Chief. I got no idea if my granddaddy knew about it or not." Hector sounded awfully defensive for someone who didn't know anything. "Less'n you got a way to talk to the dead, we ain't never gonna know, neither."

"Calm down, Hector. I was just speculating out loud, nothing more. Back to the reason we're here, I've got sensor readings for your mining ships not too far ahead."

"Yeah, I been trying to raise 'em on the company comm channel. Nobody's answering."

"What did you expect, Hector?" The Chief's voice was surprisingly gentle. "Your men got sucked through a wormhole without inertial dampeners."

"I had to try, Chief. You getting any readin' on the ship they was chasin'? That boy's debt just got a whole lot deeper."

"Why, Hector? Are you trying to say that boy led your ships into the wormhole on purpose? He had never been to Rockville

Station before. If you and I didn't know about the wormhole, how could he?"

"Didn't say he did, Chief, but he ran from my boys and my boys all ended up dead because of it."

"What the hell did you expect him to do, Hector? He heard you order your boys to blast him out of space. You'd have run, too, if you'd been in his position."

Michelle turned to me. "Why haven't they mentioned the debris from the two sleds I blasted?"

"They need to be closer to pick up stuff that small. They'll be in range soon."

Not a minute later, Hector gave a yell of triumph. "Ha! Looks like my boys got 'im before they got sucked into that wormhole. My sensors are pickin' up ship debris."

"Well hooray for you, Hector. Now you've got two more deaths to answer for."

"They killed my boy 'n I killed them. It's the way things are out here, Chief."

Our passive sensors showed the Chief's ship heading back toward the wormhole.

"And what if it turns out to be self-defense, like that girl claimed? When the telepath gets here on his circuit, do you really think he's going to read Paco's gang and find anything else?"

"I don't care what some ponce psi boy finds out. I did what I had to do, Chief."

"And I'll be doing the same thing when I arrest you for the murder of that boy and girl."

Hector laughed. "You can try, Chief, but we both know I got fifty times as many people workin' for me than you got workin' fer you."

"It ought to make for mighty interesting times, Hector." The Chief sighed. "There's nothing else for me to do out here. I'm heading back. You coming?"

"Soon. I'm just gonna blast these ships, make 'em funeral pyres for my boys."

The wormhole opened and the Chief's ship jumped away.

Michelle sighed. "Not that I doubted you, Matt, but I am glad to see that wormhole open up again."

"Me too, babe."

We watched Hector blast his mining ships and then he surprised me by reciting a prayer for the dead.

"Why did he broadcast the prayer over the comm?" Michelle asked.

"It's an old spacer tradition. Sound doesn't carry in a vacuum, so they use radio to make sure God hears their prayer."

"I like that." Michelle was silent for a bit. "After Hector leaves, we should say a prayer for them, too."

"Even though they were trying to kill us?"

"Especially because they were trying to kill us. Our words of forgiveness might help their souls to rest easier. And it might help our minds to rest easier." Michelle saw me looking at her, surprise written on my face. "I don't know about you, but I don't want to carry those men around with me for the rest of my life. Forgive them. Let them go. Get on with life."

On the sensor screen, we watched Hector's ship turn away from the wreckage. He looked to be in no hurry to jump back to his home system. Then, just before his ship entered the wormhole, something detached itself from his ship and sped away into deep space. A minute later, Hector's ship vanished, leaving just us and the mysterious signal.

"What is that, Matt?"

"Let's bring up the full sensor system and find out." I punched a few keys and got a much more detailed reading within a minute. "Now that *is* interesting. It's a messenger drone." A quick glance at Michelle showed she had no idea what I was talking about. "Messenger drones are small, unmanned spaceships used to carry messages between star systems. They're a lot cheaper than a courier ship for sending reports and mail back and forth. The military and the Scout Corps have really sophisticated drones that can make multiple wormhole jumps but this is a basic, single jump drone."

I finished bringing the engines online and began maneuvering toward the same course the drone was taking.

"Let me guess, you're going to follow the drone?"

"Got it in one, Michelle. There's got to be another wormhole on that course. The minute a properly equipped survey ship gets here, they'll discover that wormhole. Whatever is at the other end, Hector wanted to keep it secret as long as possible and send a warning through to them. I want to see what he's protecting."

"But won't Hector's buddies be suspicious when the wormhole opens?" Simply asking the question gave Michelle the answer. "No, because they'll pick up the messenger drone's signal. And we can just slip away and run dark when they come to get the drone."

As the *M&M* arced into the drone's wake, Michelle broadcast her prayer for the dead. She surprised me by including Paco in the prayer. We were quiet as I lined us up behind the unmanned ship. Ten minutes later, a new wormhole opened before us.

For the second time this day, we jumped into the unknown.

LOST AND FOUND

Our first jump into the unknown lasted close to three hours. The second jump was over almost as soon as it began. Thirteen minutes after jumping, the wormhole exit alarm sounded. A minute after that, we popped back into normal space.

A bright yellow star filled our view screen, blocking out everything else around us. The screen automatically darkened and the ship's cooling system kicked on. The proximity warning light strobed, meaning we were within fifty million kilometers of the star.

"Um, aren't we a little close to the star, Matt?" Michelle feigned nonchalance, but I heard the tension in her voice. The last eleven days traveling with me had subjected her to lots of new and not always pleasant experiences. Here was one more.

"A bit, but it's nothing to worry about. The *M&M* can take the heat for a while."

"*A while?*"

That was the wrong choice of words. "Sorry, I should have been more specific. The ship can handle these temperatures for ten hours before heat becomes an issue for her systems. We'll be far from the star by then."

To reassure Michelle, I angled the ship away from the star and increased power to the engines. To distract her, I said, "Can you track that drone? I don't want to lose it while we're getting clear of the flaming ball off the port bow."

Michelle dragged her eyes away from the view screen and concentrated on the scanners. "That's odd. The drone is holding its same course. Won't it get dragged into the star after a while?"

"Oh, that *is* clever."

"Are you going to expand on that, Matt, or do I have to guess what you mean?"

"There's no need to guess, my dear, it's just logic. I bet you can figure it out if you try."

Michelle gave me an annoyed expression, but she wasn't thinking about our proximity to the star any more. "I don't see what's so clever about losing a messenger drone and its messages because someone was too stupid to program a course away from the star."

Once again, as soon as she said it, Michelle figured it out. "It's a kind of self-destruct system. If the message's intended recipient can't get to it, the star destroys the drone before anyone else can get it." But Michelle took that line of thought one step farther than I had. "Crap! Shut everything down, Matt. Run dark *now*!"

Without another word, my fingers flew across the control panel, shutting down everything except the life support system. Michelle did the same with sensors and communication. A minute later, the air scrubbers and the passive sensors were the only systems still running.

"Now that we're running dark, Michelle, would you please explain why we had to go dark right now?"

Michelle turned a devilish smile my way. "It's just logic, my dear. I bet you can figure it out if you try."

"You turn my own words against me. How-"

"Appropriate? Fitting? Irritating?" Michelle asked.

"I'd been going to go with 'appropriate' but I'm leaning heavily toward 'irritating' now. And you can wipe that smug look off your face. I've figured it out."

Michelle propped her head on one hand. "I'm breathless with anticipation, honey."

"The drone will get pulled too close to the star to survive after just a few hours. It's an effective message self-destruct system because no ship can get in here fast enough to save the drone unless they're positioned close to the star and watching for the drone's signal. That means a ship should be here soon to pick up the drone. And if we weren't running dark, they'd pick us up on the sensors, too." I leaned back in the pilot seat and put my hands behind my head.

"Yes, you're very smart, Matt. Almost as smart as the girl who figured that out first."

"Which she only realized after the smart guy figured out the solar self-destruct procedure."

The passive sensors beeped, cutting off our one-upmanship. We both hovered over the sensor console, watching a ship match courses with the drone and then merge with the signal. We waited for the ship to pull away, but it maintained its course. Ten minutes later, the ship still held its position. Meanwhile, the temperature inside the *M&M* rose to twenty-six degrees. It wasn't much of a rise—only a couple of degrees—but the cooling system had only been off for twenty minutes.

"What do you think they're doing?" I asked.

"Sending a reply, maybe?" Michelle ran a hand across her brow.

"But why is that taking so long? Drones are dead easy to program—just upload messages, set coordinates, and turn it loose." An idea occurred to me. "Unless that crew is just the pick up and delivery team. In that case, they'd have to talk to someone with authority to find out what message to send back."

"So we're going to burn up because the evil genius sent minions to pick up messages from their crony, Hector?"

"They're going to have to hold position for more than ten hours before we need to worry about burning up."

"Yeah, but what about broiling? The temperature in here is rising pretty fast."

I didn't have an answer for her. The minutes dragged by and still the other ship maintained its position. The temperature inside the *M&M* continued climbing, passing thirty degrees after another fifteen minutes. Both of us sweated freely as the pickup ship continued to hold its position and the temperature reached thirty-five degrees.

"Matt, what are the chances that ship's sensors will pick up the cooling system if you turn it on?" Michelle's sweat-soaked clothes stuck to her body, and she looked as miserable as I felt.

"I don't know. The star might cause enough interference to mask it or the sensor tech on the other ship might miss it if he's inattentive. If it gets up to forty in here, I'll risk it."

"If they do detect us, can you restart the engines fast enough for us to get away?"

"From that tub? Sure. But we still don't know what else is in this system. And we won't know where to look for other wormholes if this system isn't on the charts."

"How far do we have to get from this sun before you can take star readings?"

"No farther than we are now, but I need full sensors. Give me those for five minutes and, if this system is on the charts, I'll know where we are."

We lapsed back into silence, sweated, and watched the sensors in the hopes the ship would leave. It didn't, and the temperature climbed steadily to forty degrees. I turned an inquiring look on Michelle. She nodded.

"Pray for solar interference," I said and switched the cooling system on.

Blessed cool air blew through the cabin and across our sweat-soaked bodies. Michelle and I took turns spinning in front of one of the blowers while the other watched the scanners for any signs the other ship had detected us. It held its position for another forty minutes. By then, the temperature in the cabin was back down to a comfortable twenty-three degrees.

"Matt, the ship is doing something." Excitement tinged Michelle's voice. I didn't blame her after the monotony of the previous two hours.

I checked the scanners. "They're probably launching a drone to carry a message back to Hector."

We continued watching as the ship's engines came to life and it gently pulled away from the object it had left behind. Once the ship was clear, a drone flared to life and accelerated toward the wormhole.

I settled into the pilot seat. "Okay, give them another fifteen or twenty minutes to get clear and we can get going ourselves."

"It's going to be sooner than that." Tension pushed the excitement out of Michelle's voice. "The ship is swinging about. They aren't pointed at us yet, but I can't imagine any other reason they'd change course."

"They must have picked up some kind of reading from the cooling system." I sighed. "Why can't that ship have a lazy captain who doesn't worry about little sensor anomalies?"

"Time to go?"

I began the emergency restart procedure. "Time to go."

Ten seconds later, Michelle announced, "We're no longer an anomaly on their sensors, Matt. The ship has gone to full engine burn and is picking up speed quickly. Are you sure they can't catch us?"

I took a quick glance at the sensor screen. "I don't think so."

"This is not a good time for a vague response, babe. Can you skip any startup steps?"

"I'll do what I can." I pointed toward a switch on Michelle's control board. "We've got enough power for the full sensor suite, now. Toggle that switch and tell me what we're facing."

Michelle hit the switch and studied the readings. "I've never seen anything like it before. It's got heavy heat shielding, really big engines, and- Uh oh."

My hands flew over my control board, skipping such trivial things as the fire suppression system and—though I hated to do it —the inertial dampeners. Saving them for later shaved thirty seconds off the startup right now, but it also meant I couldn't simply duck back into the wormhole and go back the way we came.

A garbled voice spoke from the comm then cleared. "Come in unidentified ship. Are you in distress? Hold position and we can take you in tow with our tractor beam."

"Tractor beam?" I risked a glance at Michelle.

"That was the 'uh oh.' Am I right in guessing ML tractors are military grade?"

"Uh oh." Ungainly as that ship was, if they caught us in the tractor beam we wouldn't easily break free. I skipped the next four steps in the startup procedure and hit the engines.

"Repeating, this is solar research vessel GCS-1017. Are you in need of assistance?"

My brain locked down and my hands stopped flipping switches. *"What did he just say?"*

"Matt? This is not a good time to freeze on me."

The comm crackled again. "Unidentified ship, please respond."

I gave myself a mental shake and resumed the emergency startup. "Whatever you do, don't respond to that ship."

"I wasn't planning to. But once they're in our wake, you had better tell me what spooked you."

I hit one last button and reached for the throttle. "Hold on to something. This might be rough."

Rough didn't begin to describe it. The engines rattled and shook the *M&M* as they went from cold to full thrust in a split second. I muttered a fervent prayer to the red-robed patron saint of engineering and chose a course at right angles to the course of the approaching research ship. With a lurch, the *M&M's* engines roared to life. A giant hand pressed Michelle and me back into our seats, leaving us gasping to breathe through the press of five gravities of force.

"Tractor beam's on and sweeping toward us," Michelle forced out.

"Hang on." I angled the nose of the ship down and slightly toward the other ship. The *M&M* shook as the tractor beam brushed our tail, but it wasn't enough to stop her. The other ship swung ponderously around toward our course, but by then we were beyond the range of the tractor beam and moving faster than the research ship's likely top speed.

I eased back on the throttle, giving Michelle and me a chance to breathe a little easier. As soon as I could lean forward through the g-forces, I started bringing the inertial dampeners online. Thirty seconds later, the dampeners blocked the g-forces. Michelle and I drew deep lungfuls of air and she flashed me her dazzling smile.

"Nice job getting us out of there, Matt. Though I seem to recall you claiming you could outrun that tub without any problems."

"We *are* outrunning that tub without any problems."

"Granted, but you led me to believe getting away from the ship would be just as easy."

"Um, I didn't want you to worry about something beyond our control?"

Michelle's smile vanished. "That had better be stupid guy bravado and *not* your take on 'I didn't want you worrying your pretty little head over it.' Care to try again, Matt?"

"Sorry, I didn't mean either of those. It was supposed to be a joke." Michelle's glare didn't waver, so I tried another approach. "A poor joke, obviously. The truth is I had no idea that ship would have such powerful engines. The whole design—the engines, the tractor beam, the shielding—makes perfect sense for a solar research ship. That ship needs the engines so it can go a lot closer to the sun and come back. The heavy tractor beam lets it tow large sensor arrays into and out of the heavy gravitational pull of the sun. Once they identified themselves-"

"I'm glad you brought that up. What did the captain say that made you freeze up for a few seconds?"

"The ship's identification. GCS stands for GenCo Ship." I stared out into space. "Everyone on that research ship works for me."

Michelle concentrated on the sensor control board for a few seconds. "I've started taking star readings. We ought to know where we are in just a few minutes."

"Did you hear what I said, Michelle?"

"That the people in that ship, the ones working with Hector, work for your father's company?" Michelle turned a level gaze on me. "Yes, I heard you."

"And you don't have anything to say about it?"

"What, like 'I am so shocked?'" Michelle shook her head. "After someone on the GenCo Board of Directors tried to have you killed on the maglev back on Draconis? And after Daddy told you they'd be willing to accept massive casualties just to ensure you didn't inherit and follow through with your plan to search for your parents?"

"It was my plan to liquidate my inheritance, not the search itself that pushed them to do all that."

"Was it?"

I turned away from her frank gaze, looking back after she took my hand in hers.

"Matt, you're too smart not to have considered the possibility some faction within GenCo was behind your parents' disappearance. Heck, I even brought it up back on Draconis. In that case, the last thing that faction would want is you spending billions of credits searching for your parents."

"I'd hoped I was wrong, that it was some rival company using Mom as leverage to force Dad to do research for them."

"That might still be the case, though I doubt it." The sensor board beeped and Michelle turned back to the screen. "The sensors have calculated our location. I'm feeding it to your piloting board now."

"It's the Pegasus system, isn't it?"

Michelle turned and stared at me. "How did you know?"

"A bit of logic, a bit of jumping to conclusions." I called up the system charts on the piloting console. "On the plus side, there are four charted wormholes out of here. That ought to make getting away from here easier."

"Don't clam up on me now, Matt. What made you think of the Pegasus system?"

I sighed. "The Pegasus system was the source of my family's early fortune. My great-grandfather setup a shipping and receiving station in this system and got really rich moving ore. There are still those who claim he worked with pirates to ship and fence stolen ore. Everything I've seen so far today makes me believe those stories are true."

"That's food for thought—*after* we're clear of this system." Michelle concentrated on her sensor readings. "That research ship is broadcasting something. Maybe they're calling for more ships to cut us off and round us up?"

"Can you pick up anything on the comm?"

"No, the comm is clear. They must be using a private channel."

"Scan the H band, frequencies below five sixteen. GenCo uses those for company-only broadcasts."

A few seconds later, Michelle crowed, "Got 'em. Frequency two oh one."

The comm came to life with squelches and garbled speech. Michelle sighed. "Damn, they're scrambling the broadcast. So much for figuring out what they're doing."

I flipped two switches and slowly spun a dial. The comm squawked a bit more, then, "...getting away. We almost had them. Their pilot must have skipped every safety protocol in the book to get moving that quickly."

It was the voice of the research ship's captain. Michelle turned wide eyes on me yet again.

"Corporate encryption system. Most ships only have a preset

encryption protocol, two at most. Dad and I put a master unit in the *M&M*."

A different voice spoke from the comm. "Does the ship match the description we got from Rock Jock?"

"Rock Jock?" Michelle mouthed.

"Slang for asteroid miners. Hector's codename, I guess." I responded.

"Yeah, it's a Draconis Starburst. Heavily modified, though. It's a lot faster than any fifty-year-old ship should be."

"Got it. I'll scramble some company ships that can keep up with it. They're not our guys, but they're all I've got right now. You keep tracking the ship and stay on this channel. We don't need the system authorities poking their noses into this."

"What if the ship gets past your guys and makes a run for one of the wormholes?"

"They won't. Just concentrate on your part of the plan. What's the ship's transponder reading?"

"Dammit, I should have shut off the transponder when we stopped running dark." I couldn't believe my stupidity might cost us everything.

The ship's captain replied, "There's no transponder code."

It was my turn to give a wide-eyed stare. Michelle smiled, "You were busy running the startup, so I disabled the transponder."

The other voice spoke. "That should have been part of your original report, Fred. You realize this probably means we're dealing with a Federation agent?"

Michelle and I burst out laughing. I'd love to see the guy's face if he realized he was dealing with a couple of college students.

"He could just be a smuggler, Arthur."

How generous of them to give us their names. First names only, but how many solar research ship captains could GenCo employ in the system? And how many of those were named Fred?

"We've got a solid lead for our search, Matt. You know this area best. What do you want to do with the information?"

"The *M&M* is too well known among our enemies for us to risk staying in-system. Let's get out of the Pegasus system and take stock."

"Sounds like a plan, Matt. Mentioning plans, sensors aren't reporting any other ships close by. We should take a reading on your parents while we can."

I admit it, this was my favorite part of our visits to each system. Michelle came over and straddled me in the pilot's seat. I wrapped my arms around her and kissed her deeply. We both knew this ritual was no longer necessary for me to point to my parents, but it *did* clear my mind of unnecessary clutter and gave my emotions free rein. Besides, we liked kissing each other.

After a few minutes, Michelle whispered for me to point toward my parents. As always, my arm shot out in their direction. Staying in my lap, Michelle took a directional reading then she entered the coordinates into the nav system. The nav computer added the coordinates to all the others and plotted the course.

I contented myself holding Michelle close while she entered the latest data. Her gasp pulled me from my reverie.

"What is it, Michelle?"

"The course along the latest coordinates goes right through Pegasus Station." Michelle grinned at me. "Matt, I think we've found your parents!"

THE NEXT STEP

My heart skipped a beat. Could I really be in the same system as my parents? I pushed down my rising excitement.

"It could just be a coincidence, Michelle." I tried for a light tone, but even to me my voice sounded tight.

"Yeah, that's a possibility and we definitely want to get another reading before we leave the system. But just take a look at this plot and tell me you don't think we've found them."

I leaned forward, bringing my head up next to hers. Cheek to cheek, we peered at the plotted search coordinates. The latest course blazed green against the red of older plots. The Pegasus system was within our projected margin of error for every single plot on the display. Eight other systems were also included—down from over twenty before this latest reading—but Pegasus now appeared at the center of all of the earlier readings.

I tightened my arms around Michelle. "It does look good. Let's give it an hour then take another reading."

"And what do we do if it shows your parents are on Pegasus Station? I don't think we can dock there after our run-in with the research ship."

"Even if we could dock, it might not help. The station is over twenty kilometers long and has something like half a million people living in it. Worse, the station has expanded so many times that it's like a maze inside." I sat back and considered the situation for a moment. "Pegasus Station is a good place to hold captives, though. There must be hundreds of isolated corridors and unused areas. It wouldn't be hard to block something off, making an effective little prison."

A couple of minutes later, a woman's voice issued from the comm. "GCS-1017, this is GCF-8 leading Pegasus Flight Two. Word is you've got an unidentified ship in the area."

"That's right Flight Two." It was Fred, the ship's captain. "It's currently burning hard on course oh eight six, inclination negative oh oh three."

"We'll check it out, 1017." The tone of the flight leader's voice changed from strictly formal to something more familiar. It was still business-like, but obviously directed to people she knew well. "All right, boys and girls, let's find out what's got the ship full of geeks all riled up."

Michelle asked, "I'm just guessing here, but does the 'F' in 'GCF' stand for fighter?"

"Yes."

"So you're telling me the Federation lets GenCo have its own private navy?"

"Lets? They encourage it. The Fed Navy can't be everywhere, after all. And private navies also provide a nice career path for retired military types."

"At least tell me your corporate navy is flying old, surplus fighters."

"I wish I could, but GenCo builds the current generation fighters for the navy. Odds are those are state-of-the-art warships coming after us. So whatever happens, do not even consider turning our guns on them."

Michelle flipped a couple of switches on her board. "I've retracted the guns and locked them down. There's no chance of a mistake." Michelle cocked her head. "Do you think they'll try to hail us?"

"It's standard protocol. I'm surprised we haven't heard from them yet."

"Um, Matt, the comm is still tuned to your super-secret corporate band. Turn off the encryption thing and I'll tune back to the normal comm bands."

Within seconds, the flight leader was back on our comm. "... must identify yourself. I repeat, unidentified Starburst, you have no transponder signal. Identify yourself."

"Matt, have you got another transponder ID programmed? We've got to give these people something."

"Yeah, I've got four other IDs setup." I brought up the list of alternate IDs. "Pick one."

Michelle glanced at the list and snorted. "Seriously, Matt? *Thruster?*"

I felt heat rise in my cheeks. "It seemed like the kind of thing a rich wannabe playboy might choose. I thought it might be good cover."

"It might at that." Michelle picked up the mic for the comm. "Um, hello?"

The flight leader's no-nonsense voice responded immediately. "Please identify yourself."

"I-I'm Mandy."

A man barked a laugh.

"Can it, Saber," the leader barked. Her voice took a conversational tone. "Hi Mandy, I'm Flight Commander Nancy Martin. When I asked you to identify yourself, I meant identify your ship."

"Oh! I'm sorry Nancy. Ulp, I mean Flight Commander Martin." I marveled at Michelle's act. She sounded exactly like a confused, nervous school girl.

"That's all right, Mandy. You can call me Nancy. Are you all right? Did you know your ship isn't broadcasting an ID signal?"

"Is that bad, Nancy?"

"It's illegal." In a kind, concerned voice, the flight commander asked, "Honey, you aren't alone on that ship, are you?"

"Oh no ma'am. This is my boyfriend's ship. We came over here from the Eridani system for a joy ride. He wanted to show me his rocket."

"Did he now?" Suspicion tinged the woman's voice, but it was obvious Michelle wasn't the object of it. "How old are you, Mandy?"

"Nineteen."

"Nice try, honey. How old are you really?"

Michelle heaved a dramatic sigh. "Sixteen."

"I thought so. What about your boyfriend?"

"He's twenty-four." Pride tinged Michelle's voice now. "He says I'm not like other girls my age, that I'm a lot more mature."

"Like I've never heard that one before. And do your parents know where you are?"

"Um... No. They think I'm at a sleepover." Michelle's voice went panicky. "You can't tell them, Nancy! Daddy doesn't want me seeing George as it is."

"Your father sounds like a smart man. Honey, do you understand that the spaceship is *not* the 'rocket' George wanted to show you?"

Michelle was silent for just the right length of time. "No! Did you hear what she said, George? You didn't mean *that* did you?"

"Mandy, why don't you go freshen up and let me talk to George for a minute? In private."

Michelle handed me the mic. "Uh, this is George."

"Is Mandy out of the room, flyboy?"

"Y-yes, ma'am."

"Listen to me very carefully, George, because I'm only going to say this once." The flight commander was all business again though with very heavy overtones of menace. "First, turn on your transponder *now*."

With a grin, Michelle selected the code for *Thruster*. Derisive laughter came from the rest of the pilots.

"Geez, you are one sick little bastard, aren't you?" Contempt mingled with the menace in Nancy's voice. "Second, you will now send your Federation ID to me, along with the one for that sweet little girl you've got on board."

I turned panicked eyes to Michelle, but she was already busy with her control board. She covered the mic and whispered, "I picked IDs Daddy setup for us. They'll pass."

Seconds ticked by, then the flight commander spoke again. "Yes, I can see *why* you think Mandy is more mature than other girls her age. George, this is your lucky day. I'm going to make you an offer you cannot refuse."

I didn't have to pretend to take a dry-mouthed swallow. This flight commander could be downright scary. "Okay, I'm listening."

"You're going to keep your hands to yourself and you're going to take Mandy back home. I'm going to personally escort you to the wormhole to Eridani, just in case you're thinking of making a detour." Nancy's menacing smile carried through the comm. "And I'm going to send a message through the wormhole to Mandy's father. I expect he'll be waiting for you when you dock, so don't be late."

"I- That is, yes ma'am."

"Oh, George, I just queried the age of consent on Eridani. It's eighteen. If you violate that, I will happily—joyfully, even—use some of my paid leave to come to Eridani and testify against you. Is that clear?"

"Very clear, ma'am. I will keep my hands to myself."

"Good. Now call Mandy back to the comm. I'm going to educate her a bit about men like you. If you know what's good for you, you'll respond truthfully to every question I ask of you."

For the next hour, Michelle pretended to disbelieve the flight commander. Then she pretended shock, cried, wallowed in self-pity, and allowed herself to be cheered up by her new best friend, Nancy.

Michelle had the time of her life. Me, not so much. I even had to take my second parental position reading without the benefit of Michelle's kisses. It was harder to do, but worth the trouble. It confirmed my parents were somewhere on Pegasus Station!

Flight Commander Martin—Nancy to that 'sweet little girl' Mandy—signed off with a warning. "Remember what I said, George, or I *will* hunt you down and I *will* hurt you."

"You've made that point extremely clear, ma'am."

"Make sure you don't forget it." Her tone turned much lighter. "Bye Mandy. You remember what I told you, too."

"I will, Nancy." Michelle played the ingénue to the end. "I'll stick to boys my own age and pay more attention to what my Daddy says."

"Good girl."

And then Pegasus system vanished, replaced by the foggy gray of the wormhole. I flopped back in my chair, my breath coming out in a whoosh.

"Thank God that's over. I kept waiting for something to go wrong, for that scary woman to figure out she was being conned." I grinned at Michelle. "I shouldn't have worried. 'Mandy' handled her brilliantly."

"Thank you, Matt, but I think you're doing Nancy a disservice. She's just very protective of innocents and exactly the kind of person I think you'd want in her position." Michelle picked at her sweat-stained clothes. "Is this wormhole jump long enough for me to take a shower? I must stink something awful."

"You've got plenty of time. This is a two-and-a-half hour jump." Michelle stood and headed toward the shower. Without conscious thought, I added, "Let me know if you want me to wash your back."

I didn't expect any reply, so nearly jumped out of my skin when Michelle breathed in my ear, "I want you to wash my back."

She took my hand and led me to the shower where I washed her back. I washed her front. Then we did something that would have made Flight Commander Nancy extremely angry.

Later, as we lay entwined in each other's arms, Michelle said,

"I'd always heard the first time was awkward and even uncomfortable. This was wonderful."

"That might be due to my empathic abilities. I don't think you can get any more intimate than we were. Your emotions were like sign posts, telling me where to touch and what to do." Michelle was silent, and I felt a pang of apprehension. "Are you upset I used my empathic powers during our lovemaking?"

Michelle laughed and held me tighter. "Are you kidding? What part of 'wonderful' did you not understand?"

I released a breath I hadn't realized I was holding. "When you didn't say anything after I admitted it... I just worried that you might think it was a violation or something."

"Don't be silly, Matt. I assumed you were reading me loud and clear. Like you said that was *really* intimate touching." Michelle bit her lip, her 'I'm trying to figure something out' look. "But I didn't expect to be able to read *you* when we were, ah, at our *most* intimate."

Now it was my turn to fall silent and for Michelle to ask, "Are *you* upset about that? Because I'm not. It's one thing for you to tell me you love me. It's amazing to feel your love with my body and soul!"

"Of course I'm not upset. It's just I've never heard of anything like this happening before."

Michelle's voice took on a wry tone. "And you're basing that assessment on your vast experience and training in psychic powers?"

"Good point, babe. I've read as much research as I could find on the subject, but there isn't a lot available to the public."

Michelle pulled my head down for a long, languid kiss. "Then I guess we owe it to science to research this phenomenon thoroughly."

Much later, I held Michelle as our breathing returned to normal. "I didn't know science could be so much fun."

"Classroom stuff always is boring." Michelle rolled off of me. "Everyone always says fieldwork is where the real excitement is."

"Well, this has certainly been exciting."

"It has, but now it's time to think about what we're going to do when we get to Eridani Station, Matt."

"You mean besides try to find a way to keep Mandy's father from beating me to a pulp?"

Michelle chuckled. "Yes, besides that."

"Say, where will that message the ferocious flight commander sent to Mandy's father end up? If it bounces back to her, it will give everything away."

"Daddy covered that when he setup the IDs. The message goes to a real inbox and then gets forwarded to one of Daddy's addresses. It won't bounce. Knowing Daddy, he'll even write a personal message of thanks to Nancy."

"Won't Nancy's message confuse Jonas just a bit?" I asked.

"You've known him for years, Matt. When have you *ever* known Daddy to be confused? No, he'll be pleased to get the message. We haven't been able to check in for a while, so it will tell him we're still alive and where we're going." Michelle sat up and started pulling on her clothes. "Have you got any idea what you want to do next?"

I started dressing, also. "Yeah, I've been giving it some careful thought and think I've got something."

"I hope you weren't doing that careful thinking while we were...busy."

"No, I did the thinking while you and Nancy were having your girl chat on the way to the wormhole. What we need is a reason to go to Pegasus Station and stay there long enough to find Mom and Dad."

As Michelle and I headed back to the ship's controls, she asked, "I gather it's not what you'd call a vacation paradise?"

"No one goes to Pegasus Station if they don't have to. The system has no habitable planets, and the station is for shipping and receiving, not catering to the whims and desires of pleasure-seeking tourists." I plopped into the pilot chair, noting the countdown to wormhole exit was at fifty-three minutes. "But that is our ace in the hole."

"The fact that Pegasus Station is a hellhole no one wants to go to is an advantage?" Michelle sounded dubious.

"Absolutely. When I say no one wants to go there, I mean *no one*, not even GenCo employees. GenCo *always* has thousands of job openings at Pegasus Station." I spun my chair to face Michelle. "Haven't you always wanted to work for GenCo, Michelle?"

Michelle patted my cheek. "I already do, darling. Or have you forgotten I'm one of your bodyguards?"

"And I love the way you've guarded my body today," I leered. "But you know what I meant and I think you'd make a great member of the security team."

"Okay. What are you going to do? No offense, Matt, but I don't think they're going to have an opening for company owner, empath, or all-around great guy."

"True, but I know a thing or two about computer security, having hacked your father's security systems a few dozen times. Plus, I know three different backdoors into GenCo networks." I leaned back and put my hands behind my head. "They'll hire me."

And I was right. Twenty-four hours later, traveling under yet another set of false identities setup by Jonas, Michelle and I boarded a GenCo transport to Pegasus Station.

AN UNEXPECTED PROPOSAL

Compared to the population of Pegasus Station, the new employee transport didn't hold many people. Even then, only half of its hundred seats were occupied. Out of those four dozen or so employees, Michelle was one of eight women and easily the prettiest of the group. I admit I can't look at Michelle dispassionately, but it appeared most of the other guys couldn't either. Unlike the open stares she drew at Rockville Station, the men on the transport cast furtive, disturbing leers her way. Meanwhile, the women cast openly hostile looks at Michelle.

Leaning close to Michelle, I said, "I don't like the way the men are looking at you, but I can understand it. I can't figure out what the deal is with the women, though."

"You really are clueless about women, aren't you?" Michelle smiled sweetly, removing any possible sting her words might have had. "Did you bother to check the ratio of men to women on the station?"

"No. Should I have?"

"There are four men for every woman."

"Then I really don't understand. If those women are looking for men, doesn't that make Pegasus Station a target rich environment? Even if you were looking to play the field, there would still be plenty of men left over for them."

"It's the quality of the men they're afraid I'll attract, not the quantity. A woman wants a man to choose her, not simply settle for her."

"Will it help if they see that you're off the market?"

"Maybe, but then the men aren't going to be happy with you."

"Too bad for them."

I gave Michelle a long kiss. When we came up for air, the glares of the women were less intense. But, as Michelle predicted, the men turned hostile glares on me. It made for an uncomfortable trip to Pegasus Station.

Hours later, the lot of us were herded into a large room where a middle-aged woman, who identified herself as Miss Ospin, waited. Each seat had a basic data entry station and we spent the next hour entering all sorts of personal information for taxes and insurance and stuff like that. Miss Ospin addressed us briefly once paperwork was complete.

"When I dismiss you, please proceed through the doors behind me where you will find med techs waiting to inject your ID chip into your arm. After–"

One of the very big guys, one who had glared most nastily at me, interrupted. "Nobody said nothing about putting no ID chips in me."

Miss Ospin checked her pad. "Mr. Crane, isn't it?"

"Yeah."

"If you interrupt me one more time, I will dock you one week's pay. Is that clear?"

"Um, yes?"

"Are you asking me or are you telling me, Mr. Crane?"

"Um, telling?"

She sighed and tapped on her pad. A screen lit up behind her, showing the signature page from a contract. "Is that your signature, Mr. Crane?"

"Um, yeah?"

"You're not exactly the most prized knife in the kitchen, are you Mr. Crane?" Miss Ospin muttered as she scrolled back through the contract and highlighted a paragraph. "This paragraph grants GenCo the right to insert an ID chip into your arm, Mr. Crane."

"Huh." Crane was quite the conversationalist.

"You did read your contract before signing, Mr. Crane?"

"Uh, sorta?"

"I thought as much." Miss Ospin glared at the rest of us. "I shall assume Mr. Crane isn't the only one who failed to read his contract. The ID chip serves several purposes. It controls your access to secure sections of the station, saving everyone the trouble of fumbling for an ID card. I'm told that is very difficult to do in a spacesuit. And-"

"Oh yeah, that's for sure," Crane blurted.

"That will be one weeks pay, Mr. Crane."

Crane's eyes bugged out and his face reddened. Fists balled, he rose and stalked toward Miss Ospin. Michelle jumped out of her seat and landed a kick to the back of Crane's knee before anyone else reacted. Crane wobbled and she yanked him backward, tripping him over a planted leg. As he crashed to the floor, she drove an elbow into his throat followed by a knee to the groin. Gasping for breath, Crane curled into a ball.

Two security men burst in from the door behind Miss Ospin, stunners in hand. Michelle calmly returned to her seat as Crane was dragged to his feet and marched out.

"Thank you Miss..." the woman checked her pad, "Norwood. That was very neatly done. Now, where was I?"

As if nothing had happened, Miss Ospin told us the ID chips also served as locators, helpful in a warren like Pegasus Station, as well as containing medical alerts and other data useful in an emergency.

"Is all of that clear to everyone?" When no one spoke, she continued, "Once your ID chip is inserted, you'll be directed to housing where you'll be assigned a room in the men's or women's dormitory."

"Dormitory?" one woman asked. "I don't get a room to myself?"

Miss Ospin consulted her pad, then said, "No, Miss Epps. Individual apartments are in short supply and are issued based on seniority or to married couples."

"Well what if I want to spend the night with someone? You don't expect us to just go at it in a dorm room, do you?"

"Rooms are set aside in the dormitory for such purposes. There are also several businesses on the station which rent rooms by the hour. You will have to make do with those options until such time as you qualify for your own room, get married, or complete your contract and leave. Are there any other questions?" Miss Ospin's gaze swept the room. "No? Then please exit through the doors behind me."

Everyone stood and began shuffling through the doors. As Michelle and I reached Miss Ospin, she spoke to us.

"Miss Norwood? Mr. Atwood? May I have a word with you?"

Drawing curious glances from the others, Michelle and I stepped out of line and joined Miss Ospin. She stood quietly, waiting for the last of the new employees passed through the doors.

"Miss Norwood, let me once again thank you for handling Mr. Crane."

"Please, call me Michelle. You're more than welcome, Miss Ospin."

"And you may call me Nora." She turned toward me. "Do you prefer Matthew or Matt, Mr. Atwood?"

"He goes by Matt," Michelle answered.

"You're already answering questions for him, Michelle?" Nora smiled. "Well, perhaps that's just as well."

"Just as well *what*?" I asked.

"Oh, you do speak." Nora smiled, making sure I understood she wasn't being serious. "Well, young Matt, is it a safe assumption you've noticed that Michelle here is quite an attractive young woman?"

I grinned. "Very safe, Nora. I'd have to be blind to miss it."

"Yes, and you can bet none of the other single men on the station will miss it, either. Nor will any of the single women."

"But won't they all leave us alone once they realize we're together?" I asked.

"In normal society, perhaps. Pegasus Station is not normal society. People who end up working here generally do so because they have nowhere else to go. Attractive women almost always have *some* options beyond signing on here, even if it means trading on their looks. Put simply, in the wider galaxy Michelle is a very pretty woman among many very pretty women. On Pegasus Station, it's entirely possible she's the prettiest woman here." Nora leveled an intense gaze on Michelle. "We had a woman as attractive as you arrive on station a year ago. She was lured into a dead end hallway and attacked. Her face was cut so badly, she's still undergoing reconstructive surgery. I'm told she still screams if more than two women approach her."

"I can take care of myself, Nora. You've seen that."

"I'm sure it'll take a bigger mob to really hurt you, Michelle, but it's not worth the risk." Nora placed a hand on Michelle's arm. "I have the authority to release you from your contract. You can be on the next transport back to Eridani Station, along with a healthy contract termination bonus to compensate you for your time."

"But I came here to be with Matt. I can't just leave him."

"We really need good computer security personnel, so I'll hate to do it, but I can release Matt from his contract, too."

"No, I have to stay here." Nora drew back in surprise at the intensity of my words. I temporized. "Sorry, but this is an important step in my career path. But of course, Michelle should go back."

"Oh no you don't, Matt!" The force behind Michelle's words made mine seem mild in comparison. "You are *not* shutting me out of your life now."

Nora looked back and forth between the two of us, certain she was missing something but unsure what it was. "So you're both determined to stay here?"

We both nodded.

"Very well, if you're unwilling to take my first suggestion, then please seriously consider my next one."

"Certainly, Nora," Michelle said. "What is it?"

Nora's gentle smile returned. "Get married."

"Maybe it's because I'm just a dim-witted guy," I said, "but how will getting married solve the problems you just described?"

Nora patted my arm. "I've seen your test scores, Matt. Dim-witted, you most assuredly are not. But I notice your first thought is to ask how marrying Michelle will solve the problem rather than to protest you don't want to marry her. Do you?"

"Want to marry her?" I looked at Michelle and found her watching me intently. "I didn't want Michelle thinking I was rushing into anything, so I planned to date for a while longer. And I had a much more romantic scene in mind—a crisp night on a deserted beach with a fire crackling next to us, the ring hidden somewhere she would find it... God, I don't even *have* a ring."

"But you most definitely *were* going to propose to Michelle?" Nora asked.

I glanced back at Michelle and found the same intense gaze on me. Why hadn't she said anything? "Of course."

Nora turned toward the doors behind her. "Why don't I give you two a moment alone?"

"Um, you still haven't explained why this will help keep Michelle safe."

"I'll explain that a little later. Just rest assured that it *will*." Nora pushed one of the doors open. "Besides, I think the two of you have more important matters to discuss right now."

As the door swung shut behind Nora, I turned back to Michelle. Throughout my conversation with Nora, her expression hadn't changed and it finally got to me. "What?"

"You've already planned how you were going to propose to me?" At my nod, she added, "It sounds lovely and very romantic. When did you have time to come up with this?"

"It's gone through a few revisions, but I came up with the

basics in the ninth grade." Michelle's eyes widened. "If you think that's something, you should see the ring I picked out."

Michelle ducked her head, but not before I saw her bite her lip. My heart, racing and soaring now that my plans were out in the open, plummeted. What could she be puzzling over except how to let me down gently? Her head rose slowly, she no longer bit her lip but tears glistened in her eyes.

"Matt, I can't marry you."

I tried to find something clever to say, something to hide the pain I felt. I found nothing but a gaping void where my heart had been. After a few seconds, I simply said, "Oh."

"When someone like you marries, there's got to be a prenuptial agreement. You've got to protect your family fortune and-"

I put a finger on her lips. "You mean the fortune I was prepared to liquidate to fund a search for my parents? I don't give a damn about the fortune, Michelle. But there are two things in this universe I *do* care about—that's rescuing my parents and *you*."

Michelle was determined to finish her point. "But it would look suspicious if a couple with as little as we're supposed to have insisted on a prenup agreement and your inheritance is over a hundred billion credits and... And... Oh, Matt, I'm so used to knowing exactly what to do and when to do it. But this..."

"You know what you want to do, you're just afraid it's *me* making the mistake. And *I* know I'm not making a mistake." Taking Michelle's hands, I went to one knee. "Michelle Elise Young, will you marry me?"

Michelle gazed in my eyes for the longest three seconds ever experienced by mankind and then said, "Yes."

Nora took one look at us as we came through the doors and beamed. "Let me be the first to offer my congratulations to the happy couple."

"Thank you," I replied. "Now, before we take one more step into this space station, please explain how our marriage will protect Michelle."

"It's very simple, really. The founder of Pegasus Station felt that married employees were better and happier workers. There's plenty of research supporting his opinion, but I have no idea if he was aware of it. Anyway, he instituted rules to protect marriages." Nora looked at her pad. "For example, both parties in an adulterous relationship have their contracts canceled, pay a hefty fine, and must pay for their own transportation off the station. There's a whole list of other rules, too. The end result is that people on the station simply are not willing to take the risk of pursuing a married woman or man."

"So a married Michelle isn't a threat to the other women on the station," I said.

"And a married Matt isn't a threat to the men," Michelle added.

"Like that was something to worry about," I scoffed.

Nora cocked her head and looked at Michelle, who said, "Yes, he's serious. No, he doesn't realize it."

"Realize what?" Both women laughed at my question.

"Okay," Nora said, "let's get you two married and finish your new employee processing."

The ceremony wasn't as grand as I'd assumed my wedding would be, but the end result was the same. The first thing we did as a married couple was complete the processing. It was far from romantic, but I did feel different than I had before we took our vows. Finally, with forms filled out and signed and ID chips injected into our wrists, Nora escorted us to our apartment.

"Does everyone get this level of personal attention from you?" I asked.

"Hardly, but I *do* owe your wife a debt of gratitude for handling Mr. Crane so neatly. Plus, the station guides have to take all the other new employees to the dormitories and get them settled. From the looks you two have been giving each other, I get the idea you'd like to get settled in and do a little celebrating."

It didn't take long to settle into the little apartment. It couldn't have been more than twenty-five square meters, but it had a small kitchen area, a small sitting area, and a bed.

As soon as the apartment door slid shut behind us, I kissed Michelle and swept her off her feet.

She laughed. "Why Matt, don't you want to start searching for your parents?"

"Absolutely, but I think we can spare a few minutes. We *have* just gotten married, after all."

I carried Michelle to the bed, where we spent considerably more than a few minutes.

SETTLING IN

Instead of hopping out of bed and getting right to work on finding my parents, we fell asleep. In our defense, we'd been very busy for the last several days. And all the novels and vids will tell you it's common to fall asleep after a couple of rounds of connubial bliss. Who'd have guessed the entertainment industry got something right about sex?

I awoke slowly, feeling the sense of contentment which accompanies a particularly good dream. My mind was still trying to remember the dream when it realized something was different from other mornings. I opened my eyes and found a pair of bright blue eyes staring back at me.

"Good morning, sleepyhead."

"Good morning yourself." I kissed the tip of Michelle's nose. "How long have you been awake?"

"Minutes and minutes."

"That long, huh? And you couldn't think of anything better to do than watch me sleep?"

"Nope." She sat up and swung her feet off the bed. "But now we need to get ready for our first day at work."

I hopped up and began pulling on clothes. "Right. Work. It can't be any worse than a day at school, right?"

I was so wrong it was ridiculous. My first day of work was packed with such exciting events as filling out even more forms, getting a remedial introduction to station computer security, and countless jokes about my age from the old-timers in the department. That was all before lunch. After lunch it was more of the same.

The interminable day finally crawled to an end and the CompSec team, as they called themselves, invited me to join them for a beer after work. Not wanting to alienate the people I'd see every day, I agreed.

"Just let me make a quick call." I tapped Michelle's comm code on my pad and her smiling face materialized. "Hello beautiful. You mind if I catch a beer with the guys before dinner?"

"Go ahead, Matt. I've got the same invitation from the *real* security team."

I raised an eyebrow. "Real security?"

"You know, as opposed to you lame computer security guys. At least, that's how my team leader explained it to me." Michelle giggled. "There's apparently a big rivalry."

"Maybe in the minds of *real* security. No one mentioned it up here in CompSec."

"Whatever. Have fun with your friends. First one home cooks."

"And second one home cleans," I added and signed off.

I looked up to find all the guys staring at me. "What?"

"Who was that?" asked John, the member of the team closest to my own age.

"Michelle, my wife."

"Wow, Matt. Just...wow."

Greg, my manager and one of the older guys said, "She's a very pretty girl. How long have the two of you been married?"

I checked the time. "Twenty-three hours."

Greg laughed. "Let me give you some advice, son. If someone like her is waiting for you at home, don't waste time guzzling beer with us old farts."

"She's not waiting at home. Her team asked her out for a beer, too."

"In that case, we'll hoist a few in honor of you and your lady." Greg looked at the rest of the team. "The newbie's first round is on me."

The bar was packed. That's not surprising when you consider Pegasus Station wasn't what you'd call a plum assignment. There must be other forms of entertainment beyond drinking, but drinking is easy, dulls the senses, and provides camaraderie of sorts. Certainly, my new coworkers knew a lot of people in the joint, calling out names, waving, and making straight for a particular empty table.

Greg made me sit next to him. "This is the CompSec table, Matt. All these dumb lugs know to stay clear or we'll drain their bank accounts and add black marks to their personnel records." He looked around and raised his voice. "Ain't that right, boys and girls?"

The people around us—mostly men, but there were a few women as well—raised their drinks and called out, "Aye!"

I think that's what they said, anyway. It had the sound of a well-practiced ritual. As the mugs slammed down, a waitress came by with a tray full of beer mugs. Unbidden, she put one down before each of us, including me.

"Welcome to the Wingspan Bar and Grill, son," she said. "How'd you get stuck with this bunch of losers?"

Her tone was light and everyone laughed. Greg answered, "Because he's too smart to get stuck with all those *other* losers."

Around the bar, mugs rose and voices hollered, "Aye!"

The waitress patted me on the shoulder, "I'm Dawn. Just holler if you need anything, hon."

"Thank you, ma'am," I said.

Dawn put a hand to her breast, flapping it up and down like a beating heart. "Oh my, a man with manners. I just might have to keep this one, Greg."

"You're too late, Dawn. Young Matt here has already gotten

himself hitched. He says he's been married for almost a whole day."

"Well goodness gracious, honey, what are you doing hanging out with these guys? Get on home to your wife and get some of what these boys only dream of getting." Dawn hooked a thumb at Greg. "She's got to be prettier than this guy."

"Oh she is, Dawn. She is, indeed." Greg tapped a finger on my pad. "Show Dawn a picture of Michelle."

I hesitated for a second, but the rest of the guys egged me on. When Greg threatened to pull up the HR new employee listing and get Michelle's employee photo, I gave in. A few taps on the pad and one of my favorite pictures of Michelle displayed.

Dawn took the pad from me and gave Michelle a closer look. "Well, that explains why the best looking guy I've seen in half a year ended up married so young. She sure is a beauty, hon. Now I *really* don't know what you're doing here when she's waiting for you at home."

John said, "She's not waiting for him at home, Dawn. Her new team took her out for a beer, too."

"She works in *real* security," Greg added, his tone thick with sarcasm.

Dawn looked at me. "Hey, we had a bunch of newbies in here last night telling some story about a pretty little girl beating up on a big freight hauler. That has to be your wife, right?"

I shouldn't have been surprised. A story like that gets around quickly in a place like this. "Yes ma'am, that was Michelle."

"Hey Ronnie, remember the newbies telling us about the girl that kicked ass at their orientation?" Dawn shouted across the bar. The barkeep looked up and nodded. "Turns out it's true. Matt here is married to her. And get this, she's even prettier than those guys said."

Dawn held up the pad with Michelle's photo, drawing wolf whistles and inappropriate comments from the crowd in the bar. Ronnie nodded once and went back to his duties, but Greg stood and held up his mug.

"A toast to Matt and his lovely, ass-kicking wife. May she never have need to kick *his* ass!"

Mugs raised and dozens of voices shouted, "Aye!"

I scanned the crowd, wanting to make sure I acknowledged anyone still holding up a mug. I thought it best not to ignore anyone, just in case they'd hold a grudge. I don't want any enemies stalking me when I start snooping around the station. A couple of younger guys gave me rude gestures, but their manner was genial. Just guys being guys. And there was one hard-eyed man about twice my age staring at me. When our eyes met, he raised his mug and gave a smile which never reached his eyes.

After finishing my scan and checking that hard-eyes wasn't looking my way, I nudged Greg. "Do you know everyone in here?"

Greg gazed around the bar. "Most of 'em. Why?"

"There's a guy over at the bar who was staring at me. He doesn't look like he's part of this crowd, so I wondered if he might be a friend of that guy my wife took down yesterday."

Greg easily spotted the man and waved his free hand at me. "Don't worry about him. He's been around the station forever."

"Well, who is he? Why doesn't he have a team to drink with like everyone else?"

"He's got a crew, not a team, Matt. His name is Cummings, I think. He captains one of the big research ships. Officers and crew don't mix." Greg leaned close, as if afraid the man would overhear him. "And word is most of his officers don't mix with him, either. Yeah, not many people enjoy being around Captain Fred."

That name sent a jolt through me. Had I found the captain of the solar research ship? Or, considering the hard look I'd received from Cummings, had he found Michelle and me?

One of the guys on my CompSec team asked how Michelle and I met, drawing my attention away from Cummings. The next time I looked up, Cummings was gone.

I tried not to put too much stock into that. After all, he obviously came to the bar often enough that Greg knew who he was. And the only way Cummings would know I was the pilot he'd tried to catch two days ago was if Flight Commander Martin had shown him our photos. Then I remembered Hector, Paco's father. Maybe he got a Rockville Station security vid photo of us and stored that in the messenger drone we'd followed through the wormhole to Pegasus system.

A hand waved before my eyes. "Hey Matt, you still in there boy?"

I looked up, blinking at the laughing faces around me. "What?"

Greg laughed again. "It looks like the newbie can't handle his beer. I think you've had enough for your first night, Matt."

John offered another suggestion. "He *could* be thinking about what he and Michelle are going to do when he gets home. God knows, that's what I'd be doing."

"Like you could ever get a girl, John."

John patted his pocket and we heard credits clinking. "All I have to do is walk down the corridor to the Spacer's Dream and I can *always* get a girl."

As raucous laughter burst from the rest of the team, I rose to my feet. I pretended to steady myself with a hand on the table and spoke with exaggerated care. "Greg is right—this newbie has had enough. I'm going to go home and spend some time with my lovely wife."

Being careful to knock my chair over, I called, "Goodnight everyone."

Mugs rose and the ritual "Aye!" sounded.

Just before I left, Dawn called, "You take care, hon, and bring that pretty wife of yours 'round here soon so we can all meet her."

Mugs rose again, followed by a more enthusiastic "Aye!"

Once I was away from the bar, I abandoned my tipsy act and keyed Michelle's comm code.

"Hey baby!" Michelle's voice was just a bit loud and just a bit slurred. The background noise told me she was still in the bar.

"Hey yourself." I matched her tone. "It sounds like you're still at the bar with your *real* security teammates. I just wanted to let you know I'm heading home."

"Yep, I'm still at the bar." Another voice spoke, but it was garbled in with the other noise. Laughter rose around Michelle, who said, "I can't say *that* to him!" Then she giggled and added, "Besides, he's a pretty brainy guy, so it would take a really long time to do."

Michelle's attention returned to me. "My team leader has ordered me to head home right now and...assiduously pursue amorous activities with you."

A chorus of boos came from around her. Obviously, Michelle seriously cleaned up their suggestions.

I laughed. "My team gave me pretty much the same advice, babe. See you soon. Love you!"

"Love you, too!"

I signed off and made my way home. Along the way, I added some aimless turns, stops, and starts, watching to see if anyone followed me. In the vids, the hero always spots the tail with moves like that. Real life is different. Too many people moved around me and I couldn't spot a thing. If someone *was* tailing me, all I managed to do was look like I had something to hide.

I got home before Michelle, pulled out my pad, and immediately connected through one of the backdoors into GenCo's network. I called up Cummings' personnel record, along with the records for the officers on his ship, and was deeply engrossed in those when Michelle got home. To my shame, I didn't realize she was there until she kissed me on top of my head.

"Oh no, as the first one home I was supposed to cook dinner, wasn't I?" I started to get up but Michelle pushed me back down.

She rested her chin on my head and wrapped her arms loosely around my neck. "Relax. I commed for pizza on my way home. Lizzie, my partner at work, gave me a recommendation."

I tilted my head back and kissed Michelle. "For pizza or for amorous activities?"

"Both. She says the pizza place is the best one on the station."

"And her recommended amorous activity?"

She giggled. "It sounds a bit kinky and is quite likely physically impossible."

Michelle's eyes wandered to my pad's screen and her eyes widened. She pointed to Cummings' first officer. "I saw that guy at the bar this evening."

"Was he watching you?"

"Yeah, but so were a lot of the guys in the bar."

"Then why did you notice him in particular?"

"It was the *way* he was watching me." Michelle stood and bit her lip. "The other guys watched me the way the men in Rockville Station watched me. But that guy? He'd give me this creepy, intense stare—but only when he thought I wasn't watching. Who is he?"

"He's the first officer on the GCS-1017—the solar research ship that fetched Hector's messenger drone." I flipped back to Cummings' photo. "This is Fred, the ship's captain. *He* was in my bar and watched me just as intently."

The pizza arrived and we took a break for dinner. Lizzie was right about the pizza—it was delicious. Our hunger sated, we curled up on the apartment's small couch.

"We need to memorize the faces of all the officers serving under Cummings," Michelle said. "It's a pain in the ass that they're after us because Paco forced us to kill him, but they can still derail our plans."

"Yeah, I had the same thought. I wanted to do a cautious search for my parents, but it doesn't look like we have that luxury."

"I agree. That's why I put in a call for help."

"You sent a message to Jonas?"

"I just hope he can get here fast enough to help us."

"I just hope he doesn't kill me for sleeping with his daughter."

"Why would he do that?" Michelle smiled. "After all, we *are* married."

"Yeah, but we kind of skipped a step on the road to success. After all, step one is 'finish school.'"

"Call me crazy-" Michelle began.

"You're crazy."

She smiled but pressed on. "*But* I think 'marry a billionaire' will prove to be an acceptable alternative." Michelle swept her arm, encompassing the little apartment. "And you're already providing me with this luxurious lifestyle. What more could a father want for his daughter?"

"You make a compelling argument, wife. I just hope my father-in-law accepts it."

"Well, I just hope my parents-in-law accept *me*."

"Are you kidding? They're going to love you, Michelle. God knows *I* do."

I pulled Michelle into a deep kiss. When we came up for air, Michelle whispered, "Point to your parents."

My arm shot out and Michelle noted the direction. Of course, when we overlaid it on a map, it covered almost the entire length of the station. Studying the map, Michelle highlighted several large sections.

"You don't have clearance to enter these areas." At my raised eyebrow, Michelle added, "Your job is to keep unauthorized people out of the computer network. Mine is to keep unauthorized people out of restricted places. This was all part of my first day orientation."

"Well, breaking into the ID chip software was at the top of my list, anyway. Once I get in there, I can change our access authorizations. Then the whole station will be open to us."

"Another thing I learned today is our security software tracks everyone's movement from the ID chips." She pointed at the station map. "If you can pull that data out of the security department's software, could you setup a program to plot movement for all of the ID chips on this map? Maybe we'll see a pattern—an area along our line with extremely limited access, or maybe even two ID chips that stay in a single, remote area."

"You think they'd have chipped my parents? It seems kind of risky to have them show up on security monitors."

"But what if they managed to escape? Your parents are really smart, after all. Whoever is holding them here would want to be able to track them."

"That's possible... And tracking all movement is brilliant. Let me set that up now."

An hour and a half later, I sat back from the computer and watched the first of the movement plots appear on the station map. I whooped in triumph.

From behind me, Michelle asked, "Does that mean you've got it working?"

Never taking my eyes from the screen, I said, "Yep."

"Good."

Michelle spun my chair around and pulled me onto my feet. She wore one of my shirts, with the tail dipping strategically in front and rising to show off a lot of leg on the sides. All but the bottom two buttons were undone, leaving a plunging V all the way to her navel. She looked absolutely amazing.

Pulling me toward the bed, she whispered, "Now, about those amorous activities..."

To our surprise, Lizzie's suggestion *was* physically possible.

A SURPRISE MEETING

The clatter of dishes woke me up the next morning. I rolled over and saw Michelle, already dressed in her security uniform, laying out breakfast.

"Why are you awake so early?" I sat up, stretching. "We don't have to be at work for another three hours."

"Maybe you don't, but Lizzie and I have dawn patrol today."

"You do realize space stations don't have a dawn, right?" I started pulling on clothes.

"You do realize I didn't give it that name, right? Anyway, every newbie draws a dawn patrol because some long-ago manager decided it was easier to grok—I swear to God, that's a quote from the manual—the station layout if each newbie walks their sector before it gets crowded."

"A manager of what? The subcommittee for the committee for the task force for new employee orientation and empowerment? Or was it some other ridiculous management fad? If that's what you have to deal with working in security, you have my pity."

I checked the progress of the ID tracking plot on the station map. It was slowly taking shape, with most of the nighttime traffic centered around the entertainment sectors. Everything else was too sparse to mean anything yet.

Turning away from the pad, I went to the table. Wrapping my arms around Michelle, I gave her a good morning kiss. "Mmmm. Breakfast smells good. I bet nobody reheats leftover pizza like you do."

"Pizza reheating prowess is but one of my many abilities." Michelle slipped out of my arms and grabbed a couple of coffee mugs. "Just think of all the exciting things you have yet to discover about me."

I brought the coffee pot to the table and poured. "I liked everything I discovered last night."

"Me too." Michelle's eyes sparkled over her coffee mug. "So what are you going to do this morning while I'm out grokking the station?"

"I guess I'll get busy cracking the ID chip program. I only wish CompSec software was as easy to crack as *real* security's ID tracking application."

"Are you suddenly getting into the inter-department rivalry, Matt?"

"That depends. Does it turn you on?"

"You're the empath. You tell me."

We bantered like that all during breakfast. It felt comfortably intimate. It felt right. And I missed it the moment Michelle walked out the door. I missed *her* the moment she walked out the door. So I buried my feelings the way men have done for thousands of years—I concentrated on work. And just before leaving for my own work, I cracked the ID program. I'd have to wait to modify our clearances when I got home, but the hardest part was out of the way.

My second day of work passed much like the first, though I felt more like I was part of the team. The guys cracked more jokes, asked inappropriate questions about what Michelle and I did after I got home, and were generally more at ease around me. It was like there had been a secret test and I'd passed it.

The guys didn't press the matter when I begged off joining them for beer. They did speculate freely about what I planned to do when I got home, with a couple of them offering specific suggestions. Greg even tossed out the same idea Lizzie told to Michelle the night before.

"No way, Greg," John laughed. "I'm pretty sure that's impossible to do."

I shook my head. "Wrong, John. You've got to be flexible, but it's definitely possible—and well worth the effort."

I strutted out the door, leaving my coworkers staring after me with slack jaws.

A short tube ride later, I waved the hand with my ID chip in front of the reader for our apartment. The door slid open with a quiet swoosh. Longing to be with Michelle again, I opened my mouth to call a greeting. And stopped when I saw a figure bent over the pad I'd left running the data collection routine.

He wore the shapeless coveralls and hat of station maintenance and had his back to me. Instinct told me to sneak up on him and clout him over the head—but would a typical station employee do that?

"Hey, what the hell do you think you're doing in my apartment?" Along with yelling, I stomped heavily into the room.

The figure didn't even have the grace to jump. He just straightened up and turned around. Wearing an impish grin, *she* pulled off her hat and released long, golden hair.

"Michelle?"

"I'm sorry if I startled you, Matt, but this was the best test I could think of for these coveralls."

"You've lost me. What were you testing?"

She tugged at the loose fabric at the hip of her coveralls. "That this ugly thing disguised my body. If even you don't recognize me, the coveralls will do just what we need."

"Well, it works. It completely hides one of your best *ass*ets."

Michelle smacked my chest playfully. "You're incorrigible."

"Well, those coveralls aren't going to incorrige me to give you a second glance."

Michelle's eyes rolled and she groaned. "I'm pretty sure puns like that are grounds for divorce in most systems."

"I'll take that as a compliment."

"You would." Michelle gave me a quick peck and pointed toward the bed.

Gathering Michelle in my arms, I said, "Well, if you insist."

"I was pointing toward *your* coveralls, Matt. After all, you've got *ass*ets to disguise, too."

"And we'll need these disguises for what?" Comprehension dawned. "Oh, right, moving around the station unnoticed. Good idea. Where did you get them?"

"I just stopped by maintenance, waved my chip in front of their ID reader, and told them the security team needed them for an exercise."

"Brilliant, babe." I plopped down in front of my pad. "Guess what I did this morning after you left?"

"Cracked the security for the ID chip software?"

"Yep. And, if you'll give me a few minutes, I'll grant us all permissions access."

"I have to show my ID a lot for work—is that 'all permissions' bit going to show on the screen when my chip is read?"

"Give me a little credit. I'm going to code the permissions to hide behind our regular clearance. The special clearances don't go into effect unless your normal clearance is too low."

Michelle patted my head. "Now who's brilliant?"

It took but a few minutes to make the changes to our permissions. Leaning back in the chair, I said, "Okay, there's nowhere on this station we can't enter if we want to."

Michelle tossed the coveralls to me. "Then get dressed and let's get started."

Besides the coveralls Michelle also had a maintenance data pad and box of tools. Guess who got to carry the tools?

Minutes later, we were on the tram heading out of the administrative sector. No one gave us a second look, though Michelle played the part to the hilt anyway.

She called up a station map on the data pad and pointed to the warehouse sector. "Some freight ape called in a sticking door. Karen says to get it fixed pronto." Her voice dropped slightly. "Did you know she's sleeping with Sam?"

My input wasn't really needed, so I stuck to the stock man's answer. "Huh."

"I *know*! I'd sure never have guessed those two would hook up. Karen and Joe, yeah, but Sam?"

"Huh."

"So, anyway, the door's blocking some timed delivery freight. If we don't get the door working the station might have to pay the fine. And we can kiss a raise goodbye. So fix it right the first time."

"Right."

Michelle kept that up for twenty minutes, until we got off deep in the warehouse sector. The main shift was off for the day, so there were only a handful of others working the sector. No one paid any attention as we headed into the sector.

As soon as we were completely alone, Michelle said, "Take a parental pointing, Matt."

We didn't risk a hot and heavy kiss, but I didn't need one now. I cleared my mind and pointed.

"Damn, that's deeper into the station." Michelle recorded the direction I was pointing and added it to the map with the pointing from last night. "The two lines cross maybe two kilometers from here—over near spaceship maintenance. Well, at least we're dressed to fit in with the ship techs."

We walked through twisting, turning corridors and I pointed and we mapped. Slowly, a likely sector emerged from all of my parental pointings. I tried hard to contain my excitement, but simply could not. I was less than a kilometer from my parents and the entrance to starship maintenance was just ahead.

Neither of us gave it a second thought when the door ahead of us opened. As Michelle said, we were dressed to fit in anywhere. Two women and four men, all wearing flight suits, headed our way. They were busy talking among themselves and barely noticed us.

One of the women smiled and nodded in greeting as we passed. I did the same.

Behind us, their conversation stopped. A woman's hand fell on my shoulder and spun me around. Through a predatory smile, the woman said, "Well, well, if it isn't our old friend George."

Why did this woman call me George? Then it hit me. By a stroke of fiendishly bad luck, I'd stumbled into Flight Commander Nancy Martin, someone with no love for the cradle-robbing George persona Michelle gave me when we first came to the Pegasus system.

I sought to keep this revelation off of my face and out of my voice and strived for puzzlement. "Sorry, you've got the wrong guy." I tried a smile. "I'm Matt."

"Like hell your name is Matt." Nancy's face screwed up in a snarl. "You know, George, I didn't believe Cummings when he told me he saw you in a bar last night. I figured not even *you* would be stupid enough to come back here after our little talk. But here you are—and Cummings even says you're pretending Mandy is your wife or something sick like that."

Michelle had stopped and was leaning against the wall with her back to us, acting exactly like a bored maintenance tech waiting for her partner.

Over my shoulder, I said, "Go on, Brenda. I'll catch up with you once I get this woman straightened out."

"Gotcha," Michelle replied in a husky voice. Pushing off from the wall, she sauntered toward the door to spaceship maintenance.

Turning back to Nancy, I brushed her hand off my shoulder and sharpened my voice. "Look, I don't know George, I don't know Cummings, and I sure the hell don't know you. I *do* know my boss will have my ass in a sling if I don't get my work done on time. Would you want me interrupting your work shift to talk about people you don't know?" I paused for a split second as if waiting for an answer. "I didn't think so. Now, go away and let me get on with my work!"

As I turned away, one of the guys with Nancy said, "You know, I think he looks younger than George. Less pudgy, too."

"Maybe..." Suspicion still tinged Nancy's voice. "Let me check something."

Nancy and her flight crew were silent for several seconds. I resisted the strong temptation to turn around and see what they were doing and the equally strong temptation to run. When I caught up with Michelle, she wore a tense expression—probably matching my own.

"Here we go." Nancy's voice had a satisfied tone.

"What are you doing on HR's site?"

"They always post pictures of the latest batch of newbies. He said his name was Matt, right?"

Under her breath, Michelle said, "Dammit Nancy, give it a rest. Matt, be ready to run."

"There he is." It was the other woman in the flight crew. "It does say his name is Matt."

"Yeah, but it also says he works in CompSec." The suspicion in Nancy's voice was stronger than ever. "Hey, it says he's married. Let's check the wife's picture."

A split second of silence was broken by Nancy's shout. "Come back here, you son of a bitch!"

Michelle and I sprinted down the corridor toward the slowly closing door into spaceship maintenance.

"I'm going to beat you to a pulp when I catch you, George," Nancy screamed, rage replacing suspicion. "And then I'm going to space what's left of you for what you're doing to Mandy."

Feet pounded after us as we dashed out of the warehouse sector. I scanned ahead of us, looking for an escape route.

"Keep me from running into anything, Matt." Michelle held the maintenance pad in one hand and called up a station map with the other.

I caught her upper arm and kept sprinting. Behind us, the door thunked shut but the sounds of pursuit didn't cut off. Obviously, Nancy and company got through the door before it shut. We could have used the seconds that would have bought us since our pursuers knew the sector and we didn't. Too bad the gods of chance decreed otherwise.

"Have you found a bolt hole yet, babe?" We passed several side passages, but stations had far too many dead end corridors to risk taking one at random.

"Maybe. Take the second corridor on the right." Michelle returned her concentration to running and I released her arm. "After that, take the first turn to the left and then the third turn to the right."

"Got it. I don't suppose you have any weapons with you?"

"Just a stun stick strapped to my leg. Useless against that many people. I'd give half your fortune for a blaster right now."

We cut to the right and into the corridor Michelle noted. I'd hoped for a rats warren of corridors branching from this one, but there were only three. Nancy and company made the turn just as we took the first left.

"We want the second door on the right after our next turn." Michelle gasped. "It's colored differently on the map, so I'm hoping we can get through it and Nancy can't."

Nancy had us in plain sight when we took the turn—no losing her that way. But the second door was no more than five meters down the corridor. Michelle reached it and waved her chip hand in front of the reader. It blinked red and didn't open. Grinning in triumph, Michelle waved at the reader a second time.

"No way they'll-" She broke off as the light blinked red again. Without another word, we sprinted on down the corridor.

"Dammit, why didn't it open?"

I had an idea but saved my breath for running. And I shouldn't have bothered. We rounded a corner and came to the end of the corridor. It ended in a door and Michelle immediately tried her chip. The light blinked green and the door slid open. We hurried in and shut the door behind us. I hit the locking switch and we looked around. It was nothing but a parts storage room—small and with no other doors.

A thump sounded from the door as Nancy and her team caught up with us. The lock beeped, I assume because someone outside tried to open the door, but the door remained shut.

"We've got maybe a minute before they can find someone to unlock the door," I said. "Have you got any ideas?"

"Yeah." Michelle pointed to a far corner of the ceiling. "That looks like an air shaft."

A closer check showed that Michelle was right. The lock beeped again as we pulled a heavy metal table to the corner and hopped up on it. The grating covering the shaft even had quick release catches. In seconds, I dropped it to the table.

I cupped my hands and bent over. "You first."

"Don't be stupid, Matt. The bodyguard goes second."

"You stopped being my bodyguard when you became my wife. And you're the one being stupid." Michelle bristled at that, but didn't interrupt me. "You're smaller and less likely to get stuck in the shaft. And you're better prepared to rescue me if I get caught than I am to rescue you if you get caught."

I bent over again, hands still cupped. Michelle stepped into my hands and I boosted her into the shaft. She wriggled out of sight and then called for me to join her. I jumped up, grabbed the edge of the shaft, and began pulling myself up.

Behind me, the locked beeped again and the door slid open.

"Catch that bastard before he gets into the air shaft," Nancy ordered.

Michelle looked back, eyes wide and fearful. I waved her on and whispered fiercely, "Go! Find me later."

Then hands grabbed my legs and dragged me down.

THE TRUTH COMES OUT

I crashed onto the table, my breath going out in a whoosh. As I gasped for air, hands grabbed my coveralls and hauled me off the table. A fist drove into my stomach, forcing out the little air I'd managed to draw into my lungs.

Then Flight Commander Nancy got into my face. "I cannot believe how stupid you are, George. What were you thinking?"

I only stayed up because two of Nancy's flight team held me up. I gave the only answer I could—ragged gasps for breath.

Nancy cupped an ear as if trying to hear something quiet. "What was that, George? I didn't catch it. Could you say that again?"

Through my struggle to breathe, I tried to form words. "May." Gasp. "King." Gasp. "Miss." Gasp. "Take."

"You finally figured that out, did you George?" Nancy shook her head in disgust. "Typical. Guys like you are all smooth when they're working on some innocent little girl, but-"

I shook my head emphatically. "You."

"Me?" Nancy's eyebrows shot up in surprise. "*I'm* the one making the mistake?"

Still fighting for breath, I nodded.

"Let me guess, the next thing you're going to tell me is that your name isn't George?"

I nodded again, almost able to breathe normally again.

"And you expect me to believe a story that stupid? Remember, I've seen George's and Mandy's ID photos. I could almost accept that you just happen to look a lot like George, but there is no way in hell I'll believe that your...wife..." Nancy's face twisted in disgust at the thought, "just happens to look like Mandy."

Drawing my first good breath in over a minute, I said, "I can explain, but you've got to listen to it all *and* give me a chance to show you proof."

An expression of mock seriousness on her face, Nancy whispered, "Oh my goodness, you must be a Federation secret agent working on a case of galactic importance. Will you have to kill us after you tell us what's going on?"

"Now who's being stupid?"

That question didn't go over well with Nancy. She slapped me hard. "I think you need to learn some manners." Nancy looked around at her team. "We're going to knock a little humility into George and then I think I'll take Cummings up on his offer."

I did not like the sound of that—especially the part about Cummings. "What offer?"

"Cummings has a friend who captains a freighter heading to Eridani Station soon. The friend has daughters and says he'll be happy to take you with him and personally turn you over to Mandy's father." Nancy leaned in close. "Just think what her daddy will do to you when he gets his hands on you."

With a sudden grunt, the man holding my right arm pitched forward, leaving my arm free. A dull, metallic thump sounded behind me. Electricity crackled and I smelled the sharp tang of ozone as the man holding my left arm arched his back and screamed.

Nancy stared over my shoulder in shock. "Mandy? What-?"

I didn't wait for an invitation to act. Pushing aside an unexpected twinge of guilt, I hit Nancy in the face with a left jab. She stumbled back a step and blood gushed from her nose. I stepped into a right cross and Nancy dropped to the ground. I sensed movement over my head and then Michelle landed a flying kick to the side of the head of one of the two remaining men. He staggered toward me. Grabbing his flight suit, I shoved him into the other man.

Michelle was already charging for the door out of the room. "Let's go!"

The two men crashed to the ground, with the head-kicked one landing on top. As I chased after Michelle, the remaining woman blocked the door. She struck a fighting stance, obviously thinking she only had to delay us for a few seconds before the others could come to her aid. Michelle dove to the floor and rolled. As she came up, she shoved the stun stick into the woman's stomach. With a scream, the woman fell to the ground, twitching. Pounding out the door, I paused just long enough to wave my ID chip across the reader, shutting it behind us.

We reached the first intersection where I expected Michelle to turn left, back the way we'd originally come. She turned right and, short of breath for asking questions, I followed. She ducked into the first corridor we came to and pulled up against the wall.

"Why-?" I began.

Michelle put a finger to my lips then pulled out her pad. Calling up the station map, she tapped for directions and surprised me by entering our apartment as the destination. I raised my eyebrows in question, but the sound of footsteps drew our attention.

"We're almost there, Spitz. Take that hall on the right." I recognized the voice. It belonged to Fred Cummings, captain of the solar research ship.

"You think we can talk 'em into giving the guy to us without making 'em too suspicious?" I didn't recognize the voice, but Spitz was the name of Cummings' first officer.

"That's already taken care of. I told naive Nancy we'd send him to Eridani Station and turn him over to the girl's father."

As the voice faded, Michelle and I left our hiding place and followed the directions back to our apartment. We'd taken two turns when we heard Cummings' cry echo down the corridors.

"What the hell happened in here?"

We took that as our cue to run some more.

We reached the tram safely and, breathing hard, settled in for the ride back to the residence sector.

"That couldn't have gone any worse." Michelle's shoulders slumped with fatigue and dejection.

"I don't know. It wasn't *all* bad." I took the maintenance pad from Michelle and connected to the network through one of my backdoors.

"Nancy is out to get you. Cummings is out to kill us. And they both know where we live. I don't see a positive."

"We found a door neither of us could open."

Comprehension dawned on Michelle's face. "I was so busy trying to get away from Nancy, I missed the meaning of that. Every door in the station should open to our new clearance."

"Exactly. We never had a chance for me to take a pointing, but if we can get through that door..." I left the sentence hanging and concentrated on the pad.

As I expected, Michelle expanded on my speculation. "That still leaves us with a couple of problems—opening that door and staying free long enough to do it." She bit her lip, gazing at the floor of the tram for a few seconds. "There's a pretty big vagrant population on the station. Maybe we can hide among them." She caught me staring at her in surprise and grinned. "That's the second thing they teach you in Real Security 101, Matt."

I couldn't help myself from asking, "What's the first thing?"

"Where to find the bathrooms in your patrol area." Eyes twinkling, she leaned over and looked at the pad. "What are you doing in the housing database?"

"Looking for empty apartments. If the situation gets desperate, we can join the vagrants, but that has its own difficulties. I'll need time to figure out how to get through the door that wouldn't open and privacy so I can leave my chip tracking program running."

"Are you hoping to identify people who can open that door?"

"You got it in one, babe." I squeezed her leg. "Plus, a beauty like you will stand out like a sore thumb among the vagrants."

"Oh, I can take care of that problem with some makeup and the right clothes." Michelle bit her lip again. This was turning into quite the day for problems. "But do you know what will happen when we don't show up for work tomorrow? It's bad enough we have Nancy and Cummings looking for us. If the whole station is alerted, an already tough mission will become nearly impossible."

That hadn't occurred to me, but I had no immediate answer. I sighed, "We can think on it after we get to our new place." I showed her the station map. "I found four empty apartments in this sector. We're taking the one at the end of the hall. I blocked it in the database, so housing won't assign anyone to it, and coded the door to open *only* for us."

"I'll bet that's how that door in spaceship maintenance is secured—coded to specific people instead of clearance levels."

I nodded. "That makes it all the more important to keep the ID plot running—so we can find out *who* those people are."

Half an hour later, we entered our new home.

Two minutes after that, Michelle and I finished moving into our new apartment. Most of that time went to setting up my pad, then I tossed my clothes onto a nearby chair. I turned to find Michelle glaring at me, arms crossed, hips canted, and one foot tapping. There must be some kind of special training class for women where that is taught because every woman I know—from Mom to Aunt Tess to teachers to Michelle—has that look down pat.

"What?"

She pointed to an open drawer. Her clothes were neatly arranged within, leaving plenty of space for mine.

I stuffed my clothes into the drawer. "I, um, wanted to make sure my clothes were within easy reach in case of an emergency?"

"A likely story." But Michelle smiled as she said that. Then she flopped back onto the bed. "I know we need to figure out what to do next, but my mind is spinning too fast to think properly."

"I know what you mean." I flopped down next to her. "What can a husband and wife do that's relaxing and doesn't take conscious thought?"

"Gee, Matt, I don't know. Do you have something in mind?"

"I do, but we're both horribly overdressed for it."

Laughing, Michelle straddled me and pulled off her shirt. "Does that help?"

"It's a start." I pulled her down and kissed her.

Later, Michelle lay next to me, idly running her hands through my hair. "I guess it's time to start thinking about what to do next."

"My mind is awhirl with possibilities." I pulled Michelle into another kiss. "But none of them involve getting dressed."

Much later, we got dressed and settled down to plan our next move.

"I think I know what we need to do, Matt. Or, at least what to consider first."

"We just sat down and you already have an idea? Don't tell me you were *thinking* the whole time."

"Did I look like I was thinking? Did I bite my lip even once?"

"You nibbled on my lips, among other things, but I see your point. So, what's your idea?"

"We need to arrange for a leave of absence from work and then make it look like we left the station."

"Why can't we just make it look like we left the station? I'm sure the company has had people skip out on their jobs before. Our bosses will be irritated, but that's about it."

"No, our bosses will follow the absent-employee checklist." At my blank look, Michelle shook her head. "It's a good thing I got a job in *real* security where they go over these things. First, the manager tries to comm the employee. If they don't answer, the manager should immediately request a sensor sweep of the station, looking for the employee's ID chip."

"Isn't that a bit hasty? What if the employee just forgot his comm?"

"It's a safety precaution. The employee might be hurt, in which case they can send help."

"Okay. It'll take a while, but I can set the system to overlook our ID chips. Then they'll actually believe we left the station."

"Which is worse. The station could just have a disgruntled employee running out on the job or they could have a saboteur on their hands. Security can't know which, so the whole station is locked down while Security uses ID chip data to track every move the potential saboteur made during the previous week."

"Oh. Yeah, that would be bad. So, what do we do?"

"We find someone who knows us, has at least some level of authority, and then we tell them the truth."

"That narrows the list down to Nora in HR, your manager—Tanya, right?" Michelle nodded. "Or Greg, my manager."

"Tanya is out. I have no doubt she's honest, but she's strictly by-the-book. If we told her, she'd insist on taking the story all the way up the chain of command. What about Greg?"

"He seems pretty easy-going, the kind of manager who leaves you to do your job."

"Can you trust him?"

"Maybe. Let's see what we can find in his HR file."

Thirty minutes later, Michelle and I agreed we could trust Greg. He'd been with GenCo for over thirty years, coming to Pegasus Station after his wife died. He had a clean record and his subordinates thought highly of him.

"It's just surface stuff, Matt, but Daddy taught me to pay attention to it. Criminals can hide their true nature for a while, but not for more than thirty years." Michelle stood up and stretched her back. "Next time we steal an apartment, let's pick one with newer chairs."

Stretching as well, I pulled out my comm. "Agreed."

Greg answered on the second buzz. From the noise, he was still at the Wingspan.

"Hey, Matt. I thought you were spending the evening with that pretty wife of yours. You're not bored with married life already, are you?"

"God no, Greg, but I do have a problem I need to talk to you about."

"Sure. You want to come down here to the bar or you want to meet somewhere else?"

"Does Dawn have a private room we can use?"

That seemed to catch Greg by surprise. "Yeah, I think so. Meet me here and, if it's not available, we can go somewhere else."

Michelle stuck her head next to mine and Greg brightened up. "Hi Greg, I'm Michelle. I know this is going to sound weird, but is Captain Cummings down there? Or any of his officers?"

Greg knitted his brows. "Does Cummings have something to do with all this secrecy?"

Michelle nodded. "Everywhere I go, I seem to run into one of them."

"I see." Greg looked around the bar. "I don't see any of them. You and Matt hurry on down here and we'll get this whole thing sorted out."

I thumbed off the comm unit. "That was a good idea, asking about Cummings. It never crossed my mind."

Michelle patted my cheek. "It's a good thing you have me to think of these things for you."

Michelle tossed my coveralls to me. They weren't much of a disguise—especially after our run-in with Nancy—but they disguised Michelle better than anything else we had. Twenty uneventful minutes later, we walked into the Wingspan Bar and Grill.

No one gave us a second glance. We disappeared into the background so well, I had to tap Dawn's shoulder to catch her attention.

She gave me a cartoon-like double take. Keeping her voice low, she said, "Good to see you again, Matt, and to meet your wife. Come on, I'll take you to Greg."

Dawn led us down the hall past the restrooms and opened a door. Inside was a small office piled with paperwork and barely big enough for the four of us.

"Greg, there's a buzzer right over there." Dawn pointed to a switch. "It sends a signal to the bar. Push it and I'll come back and see what you need."

Dawn bustled away and Greg shut the door to the office. With a sigh of relief, Michelle removed her hat and let her hair tumble free.

"Matt, your pictures don't do justice to this young lady." Greg sat down behind the desk and leaned forward. "So, what's this about? And don't say it's about Cummings stalking Michelle. There may be some truth in that claim, but she'd be reporting this to *her* superiors if that was the real issue."

"You're right, Greg. Cummings is part of it—and he's the main reason we came to you—but he's just part of the problem." I paused for a moment and looked at Michelle. "What should I tell him?"

Greg spoke before Michelle could say anything. "Tell me the truth. And if you don't know where to begin, start by telling me where you got your false ID cards."

NEW ALLIES

G reg's statement hung in the air for a few seconds. Michelle and I, stunned at this revelation, exchanged glances.

Turning back to Greg, she asked, "How did you know they were fakes?"

If there wasn't a desk between them, I could imagine Greg patting Michelle's head. His patronizing smile was more than enough. "Child, I've been doing this sort of thing since long before you were born. Your IDs are good—the best I've seen—but false IDs are designed to get people through casual checkpoints. They cannot withstand the level detailed scrutiny I gave them."

I leaned forward and locked eyes with Greg. "If you knew the IDs were false, why didn't you just turn us in? And what made you check them in the first place?"

"I check the IDs of every new hire in CompSec. A person can do a lot of damage from the inside of my department. When your ID came up false, I checked Michelle's, too." Greg leaned back, keeping his eyes locked on mine. "I didn't turn you in because Nora—the woman who ran your orientation—likes you. She is an excellent judge of character."

Michelle put her hands to her head and looked at the ceiling.

"Is there anyone on this station who doesn't know we've got false IDs?"

"I didn't tell Nora about your IDs. Since she spoke with you about personal matters, I just asked her opinion of you two. Did she feel you really loved each other? Was Matt just looking for a way to sleep with such a pretty girl? Was Michelle trading on her looks to get in with someone in CompSec?" Greg laughed at our expressions. "The best security person is one capable of imagining the worst in people."

"And Nora reassured you?" I asked.

"Somewhat. *She* believes you're a young couple in love. She caught something of a fugitive air about you, but in a benign way. I picked it up, too, and we talked about it. Our best guess is that Michelle's family is wealthy, Matt's isn't, and Michelle's parents are trying to keep the two of you apart."

Michelle and I couldn't help it—we burst out laughing.

Greg shrugged. "It's a bit romantic, but old folks like Nora and me like to see a little romance in the world. I guess we were wrong."

"Not entirely, Greg," I gasped out through laughter. I fought to stop laughing, but Michelle's continuing giggles interfered. "I'm the wealthy one and my parents haven't met Michelle since she was twelve."

Greg scratched his head, confused. "You ran off before giving your parents a chance to meet the love of your life?"

"No, I ran off *to* give my parents a chance to meet the love of my life."

"You've lost me, Matt."

Michelle took my hand. "Matt and I came here to find and rescue his parents."

Greg looked back and forth between the two of us. "You're serious?"

It was the moment of truth. "Greg, are you familiar with the names Richard and Angela Connaught?"

His eyes widened. "Anyone who's worked for GenCo as long as I have knows who they are."

"My real name is Matthew Connaught. I'm their son."

"Can you prove any of that, Matt? Because the news says Matthew Connaught was kidnapped."

"That's a cover story planted by my father."

"And your father would be?"

"Jonas Young, the man in charge of Matt's security detail."

Greg looked my way. "You rate an entire security detail?"

Michelle rolled her eyes. "Oh come on, Greg. Do you have any idea what Matt's net worth is?"

"Assuming he really is the Connaught heir, I concede your point," Greg said. "So where do you come into all of this, Michelle? Did you meet Matt at some Bring Your Daughter to Work day or something? I mean, I'm sure the head of Matt's security detail is well paid, but not enough to travel in the same social circles as the Connaughts."

"Have you ever heard of the Phillips School on Draconis?" I asked.

"My wife and I lived on Draconis for nearly twenty years. She's buried there, in fact. Yeah, I've heard of the school—top notch education from preschool through college. And I'm not surprised *you* went there, Matt, but there's more to getting into that school than having the money to pay the tuition. It takes connections of the kind well beyond even the best head of security."

"You're right, the Phillips School was completely out of Daddy's reach." Michelle took over the story. "Matt's father got me into the school *and* paid my tuition."

"That's quite an employee benefit." Greg sounded skeptical. "Why would he do something like that?"

"The school provides its own security staff, so bodyguards aren't allowed in the school. Matt's father believed someone was plotting against him and his family. He got me into the school to act as Matt's bodyguard when he was away from his official bodyguards."

"No offense, honey, but I'm supposed to believe a pretty little thing like you was Matt's bodyguard in school?"

"Stop patronizing my wife, Greg." Greg drew back at my angry retort. "Did Nora tell you about the big guy Michelle took down during orientation? Do you want me to tell you how she rescued me from a street gang just a few weeks ago?"

"Well, any doubts I had that you love this girl are gone. Only a man defending his woman gets that angry." Greg held his hands up in mock surrender. "Michelle was your bodyguard in school. Got it."

"Your first thought is not entirely wrong, Greg. I always carried an emergency beacon in school. Daddy trained me to set off the beacon and then get Matt into hiding while his bodyguards swarmed in from just outside the school."

"Okay, there's enough evidence that you know how to handle yourself in a fight that I'll accept the bodyguard part of the story." Now Greg turned his skeptical gaze on me. "But I'm still not convinced of your part of the story. Maybe you're a rich kid, but Connaught rich? That's hard to swallow."

Who could blame him? I lived the story and found it far-fetched even to me. "On Draconis, I could call up the school on the net, show you lots of pictures, my grades, stuff like that. Out here? I have no idea. Can you think of anything that will convince you?"

"Yeah, there's one really simple method you haven't mentioned." Greg steepled his fingers and looked back and forth between the two of us. "What I don't know is whether you're avoiding it like the plague or just haven't thought of it."

"Haven't thought of *what*, Greg?" I threw my hands up in exasperation. "I've never had to prove my identity before, so tell me already."

"He wants to do a DNA test, Matt. All corporate facilities must keep those records on file and up-to-date. As a dependent of employees, your DNA is on file." Michelle turned to Greg. "That *is* your simple method, right?"

Greg nodded.

"Fine. Let's do it and get on with rescuing my parents."

Greg gave me a thoughtful look then stood. "HR has the equipment we need. Am I right in assuming you're willing to trust Nora to do this?"

"I am. What do you think, Michelle?"

She nodded and the three of us filed out of the office. We took two steps down the hall toward the bar then Dawn scurried in from the bar.

"Get back in the office!" Her fierce whisper barely rose above the crowd noise. "Cummings just walked into the bar and brought all his officers with him."

The three of us backtracked into the little office. Dawn crowded in behind us and turned a maternal look to Michelle.

"Is Cummings stalking you like Greg said?"

Greg spoke up before Michelle could answer. "We didn't get to that part of their story yet. Why?"

"He's asking for these two—says he knows they came into the bar just a few minutes ago." Dawn pointed to the coveralls. "Those things hid you pretty well, but it won't take Cummings long to find someone who remembers a couple of maintenance techs coming back here. He'll put two and two together."

"He won't have to put anything together—he already knows about the coveralls." Michelle ran a hand through her hair. "I'm sure Nancy told him all about it."

"Who is Nancy?" Dawn looked perplexed.

Greg shook his head. "Worry about that later. What happens if Cummings gets his hands on you?"

I took Michelle's hand. "He'll smuggle us onto a ship and, if we're lucky, throw us out an airlock."

Greg stared at me, astonished. "Are you serious?"

"Absolutely. And if he finds out you've been shut up in here with us, he'll add you to his list, Greg."

Greg and Dawn both paled. "How is Cummings going to figure out I've been with you?"

"The same way he knows the two of us are here. Someone is using ID chips to track us."

"Chip tracking is one of the most secure systems in the network. I don't even have access to it." Greg gave a firm shake of his head. "Matt, you keep talking about death threats and missing parents and secret identities. And now it's Cummings cracking the ID tracking system? Son, you just sound like a crazy conspiracy theorist."

I pointed to a pad sitting on the desk. "Dawn, is that thing hooked up to the network?"

"Of course."

I spun the pad around and started tapping out commands. "Do you know anything about the chip tracking software, Greg?"

"Yeah, I maintain it. But the network director grants me temporary access every time I update it. There's no way to get into it otherwise."

With a flourish, I entered one last command and turned the pad to face Greg. "You're in CompSec, Greg. You know there's no such thing as a completely secure system."

"Holy hell, boy, how did you get this level of access?"

"Worry about that later. How many active processes run in the chip tracking system?"

Greg answered without thinking or taking his eyes off the pad. "Six. But I see eight running right now."

"The next to last process on the list is mine." I held up a hand when Greg opened his mouth to speak. "Again, I'll tell you all about it later. Can you learn anything about the eighth process?"

We all jumped a bit as the wall comm buzzed. Dawn waved us to be quiet. "That's the comm to the bar. Let me see what Ronnie wants."

Tapping the comm, she asked, "Yes, Ronnie?"

"Cummings."

"Tell him I'm busy."

"Did. Insists."

"Fine. I'll be right there." She keyed off the comm. "I don't know what this is all about, but why don't we just call security? You're one of them, Michelle. They'll show up in force."

"No!" Michelle and I said at once.

Michelle caught Dawn's arm. "I trust the people in security and they'll try to help, but it will be big and noisy and it will get people killed. Please keep them out of this—at least for now."

Frowning, Dawn nodded and walked out. Through all of this, Greg tapped away on the pad. A few seconds later, Greg smiled and leaned back, though he kept entering commands on the pad.

"That will keep Cummings busy."

"What did you do?" I craned my neck to see the screen.

"I just did a little mix-and-match with your ID signals. A couple of people wandering by the bar are now reporting as you two and you two are showing as those two people." Greg stopped entering commands. "And now the signal will swap to random nearby people every minute. That will keep Cummings and his crew busy for a while." He steepled his fingers and looked at Michelle and me. "While we wait for them to scatter, you have time to tell me everything."

So we told him everything, only leaving out my psychic ability. I'll say this for Greg, he listened carefully and asked intelligent questions for clarification.

"That's quite a story. From the way the two of you took over the story from each other, it's either true or very well-rehearsed."

"Doesn't the backdoor into the network lend credence to our story? You've used it, so you know it isn't made up."

"The best conmen build their lies around a solid core of truth. You could have stumbled across the backdoor or been friends with a child of someone familiar with it. Or you could be the best hacker I've ever met and installed it yourself."

"But–"

Greg held up a hand to stop me. "*But* this is so simple to verify that I'm withholding judgement until that DNA match is complete. And mentioning that, the way to HR should be clear. Let's go."

Michelle and I donned the overalls and we set off.

Dawn came to us when we returned to the bar. "The strangest thing happened. Cummings ranted away at me about where I'd hidden you until he got a comm call. After the call, he and his men rushed out of here. You know anything about that?"

"A bit, Dawn," Greg smiled. "Do yourself a favor and forget these two were here tonight."

Greg hurried us along little-used corridors, scouting heavily trafficked ones before leading us through them. When we left the entertainment sector, avoiding people got easier. Fifteen minutes later, we entered the station HR offices and found Nora waiting for us.

"You've been awfully mysterious about all this, Greg. Is there a problem with the station's cutest pair of newlyweds?"

"You could say that, Nora. One way or another, these two are in serious trouble. How much and what kind of trouble depends on what you discover." Greg looked around at the small staff in the front offices. "I'll say more in private."

Nora nodded and led us deeper into the office. Being in HR, she must deal with privacy requests all the time. We ended up gathered around a small conference table in a comfortable office.

"Now, what can I do for you?"

"Run a DNA scan on Matt."

Nora's eyebrows climbed in surprise and she resolutely shook her head. "Absolutely not. I cannot do a scan without legal justification. By Federation law, that's an unreasonable search."

I only saw one way out of this. "I give you permission to perform the scan and will sign whatever forms you require to grant authorization."

Nora cocked her head in thought. "You realize anything I discover is valid evidence in a court of law. In fact, the results of all scans forward to the Federation automatically."

"I knew the first, not the second. Is there a Federation consulate on the station?"

"No, the nearest one is on Eridani station. Does this information change your mind?"

I looked at Michelle, who took my hand and shook her head. "No, but it changes my timetable. How much time have we got before the Feds descend on the station?"

Nora drew back and glanced nervously at Greg. "Is he a terrorist or something?"

Greg shook his head. "Not according to his story. Tell her, Matt."

I took a deep breath. "Here's the short version. I'm Matthew Connaught, supposedly kidnapped heir to the Connaught fortune and the single largest holder of GenCo stock. The Feds will come in force because of the kidnapping cover story and because I'm a billionaire. Michelle and I are here because my parents, missing and presumed dead by everyone else, are alive and being held on this station. We're here to rescue them."

Nora blew out her breath in exasperation. "For God's sake, Greg, you're getting too old for practical jokes."

"I'm not joking, Nora. And the more I observe Matt, the more I believe he's not joking, either."

Michelle leaned forward. "Nora, just run the test for us. Please?"

"Michelle, did he feed this story to you to get you to marry him?"

Michelle leaned back and slid an arm through mine. "I've known Matt for years, Nora. I already know the truth."

Nora looked at each of us in turn then went to her desk. Grabbing her pad and a stylus, she returned. She tapped through a menu then slid the pad in front of me and handed me the stylus. "Sign every highlighted field. You're Matt Atwood until I say otherwise."

I got busy signing while Nora waved her chip across the reader on a locked cabinet. She came back with a small device, inspected the forms, and then motioned for my left hand. She held the device to my finger and I felt a sharp prick. Heading back to her desk, Nora plugged the device into her pad and tapped away.

"Connaught. Matthew. Middle name?"

"Bernard," Michelle answered.

Nora smiled. "I see she's still answering questions for you, Matt."

"She does a lot of other things for me, too."

Nora glanced at Greg. "Why do young people always feel compelled to bring their sex lives into every conversation?"

Before anyone could respond, Nora's pad beeped. She glanced at the pad and then gave me a hard look before smiling. "Would this be a bad time to ask for a raise, Mr. Connaught?"

Greg flashed a brief smile. "So the DNA scan is a match?"

Nora nodded and then looked concerned. "Please forgive my flippant way of announcing that, Mr. Connaught. Considering the circumstances, it was thoughtless of me."

"Nora, I'm still the same guy you advised to marry Michelle a couple of days ago."

"I-I'll try to see you that way, Mr. Connaught."

"And let's start by cutting out that 'Mr. Connaught' stuff. I'm just plain old Matt." I gave Nora my best friendly smile.

"Matt. Right." Nora flashed a brittle smile. "Of course, I was only joking about the raise."

Greg piped up, "Well, I'll take a raise if you decide to hand some out."

I looked back and forth between the two of them. Both were nervous, though Greg hid it better. "Look, I really am the same person I've always been. None of that changed just because you learned my real name. As for raises, you should know there's a sizable reward for assistance leading to the safe return of my parents. Once my parents are safe, you two can have the reward."

Greg and Nora exchanged glances, then Greg asked, "How sizable?"

"A quarter of a billion credits."

Nora flopped back in her chair, incredulity written on her face.

Greg blew out his breath with an audible whoosh. "That was 'b' for 'billion,' right?"

"Absolutely. Trust me, my family can afford it." I stood up and started pacing. "But first we've got to rescue my parents. Greg, pull up plans for Pegasus Station. I'll show you where we believe my parents are being held."

Nora reached for her desk comm. "While you're doing that, I'll call security."

"No!" Michelle and I, joined by Greg this time around, shouted at the same time.

Nora actually jumped at our reaction. "Why ever not? They're far better prepared to handle this sort of thing than we are."

"If we knew who and what we were up against, I'd agree with you," Michelle said. "But we don't know any of that. We can't bring security into this without making some noise—and noise could cost Matt's parents their lives."

"In case you hadn't noticed, Michelle, the four of us aren't a crack commando team. At the very least, Greg and I will be useless in a fight."

"Speak for yourself, Nora. I can take care of myself in a scrap." Greg might have been more persuasive if he hadn't sucked his belly in before speaking.

"We need you two to stay right here." Michelle pretended not to notice Greg's relief at her announcement. "Nora, if things go seriously wrong you can call security for help. Greg will use security cams to scout ahead for us and the chip tracking software to keep Cummings and his officers out of our hair."

"I see." Nora radiated disapproval. "And are the two of you crack commandoes?"

"Not exactly commandoes, but I've got extensive training in this sort of thing."

Nora threw up her hands. "I give up. Make sure to give me a list of your next of kin before you leave. I'll need to know who to alert when you get yourselves killed."

"That's getting into the spirit of the adventure, Nora." I gave her a thumbs up. "Remind me to authorize a big pay raise before we leave, too. I don't want you losing out entirely if we end up getting killed."

Nora frowned at me, but her eyes had a bit of sparkle. "All right, boss, I have a different question; one which requires a real answer."

"Shoot. Metaphorically speaking, of course."

"Is there anyone nearby we can call if you get into real trouble? Someone here on the station, I mean."

That question caught me by surprise. "Uh... I've got nothing. Michelle?"

Without even pausing to think, Michelle said, "My partner, Lizzie, and Flight Commander Nancy Martin."

I nodded my agreement. "Those are good suggestions, but tell Nancy who Michelle and I are *before* you send her to help us. Otherwise, she might space me before we can explain the situation."

Nora's eyebrows climbed to her hairline. "I can't tell this Flight Commander anything unless you tell me first. You can make it brief, but tell me your story now."

Michelle launched into the story, leaving me free to check out station plans with Greg. I showed him the non-opening door we'd found in ship maintenance and then Greg began searching through the system for access codes to it. By the time Michelle wrapped up our story, Greg threw in the towel.

"I can't find any codes for that door and I can't find any plans showing what's beyond it."

"What if we can find someone who has access to the door? Will that help?"

"Probably. I'd just have one set of permissions to check, anyway."

I took over the pad and setup a remote connection to the pad back in our borrowed apartment. "I've been plotting the movement of every ID chip for the last day. Let me narrow it down to just the area around the door."

I tapped away for a minute and the display zoomed in to a ten meter circle centered on the door. A lot of people passed by the door, but two ID signatures came to the door and just vanished. One of them reappeared outside the door three hours later. The second one was gone for nine hours. From there, Greg easily identified the owners of the two chips.

The ID chip which disappeared for nine hours belonged to a freight handler named Alfred Morgan. Nora called up his HR file while Greg fished out the identity of the other person.

"Well now, that *is* interesting." Greg leaned back and looked at me. "It appears your nemesis Fred Cummings is in this deeper than you thought."

"Cummings is connected with those hidden wormholes and Hector from Rockville Station. How can he be in on my parents' kidnapping, too?" I shook my head. "It doesn't make any sense."

Nora looked up from Morgan's HR file. "I'm sure it makes perfect sense, Matt. You just don't know the facts that connect everything."

"Well, it's past time to start figuring it out. How much time do you think we have before the Federation offices on Eridani Station get the results of my DNA scan?"

"Seven or eight hours. Say an hour to organize a response team, two and a half hours in the wormhole." Nora ticked off hours on her fingers. "Call it ten to twelve hours."

"We'll call it nine," Michelle said. "Daddy taught me to *always* plan for less time than I expect to have." Michelle turned to Greg. "You and Matt said those IDs just vanished at the door. Do you have any idea what could cause that?"

"Some kind of electronic shielding, I'd guess. If you can find a way to turn it off, we'll be able to actually help you out when you're beyond the door."

Michelle nodded. "Matt, we're depending on you for that. I don't have the technical background for it. Nora, is there any way I can get my hands on weapons? We left our blasters on board our ship, which is docked back at Eridani Station."

"People sometimes get a bit rowdy here in HR—as you saw during the orientation—so we keep some stun sticks and tasers on hand. I can give you both one of each."

"It'll have to do." Michelle turned back to Greg. "Can you give Matt and me the same permissions Cummings and Morgan have while leaving all our existing permissions in place?"

"Already done, Michelle."

Greg stood as Nora pulled our weapons from the same locker which held the DNA scanner. We pulled our coveralls on again. I stored the taser in a pocket and pushed the stun stick up my left sleeve.

Greg shook my hand and gave Michelle a hug. "Good luck, kids. Be careful."

Nora hugged both of us. "I'll be praying for you two. And for your parents, Matt."

We had nothing else to say. With a half salute, Michelle and I headed off to rescue my parents.

OLD ENEMIES

Walking out of HR, Michelle and I dialed up a comm connection with Greg so he could help us avoid Cummings and his men.

"I don't know how useful I'm going to be, kids," Greg told us. "I still show you two bouncing all around, from one ID chip to another, but I called up tracks on Cummings and his officers. They've broken up into pairs and have scattered all around the entertainment and housing sectors of the station."

Great. Our path to ship maintenance went right through those two sectors.

"Looks like they figured out they were chasing ghosts. We can't really complain, since it let Michelle and me get to Nora's office unseen."

Michelle pulled up the station map on the maintenance pad. "Is there another way we can go that won't take too long? I'm not seeing much on the map."

"Let me check."

We heard Greg tapping on the pad then heard Nora say, "Give me that thing, Greg. I've got an idea."

"Kids, Nora wants to talk to you, so I'm handing it off to her."

We heard clacks and taps as Greg and Nora fumbled with the

comm, then Nora spoke. "Do you two remember when you got to the station two days ago?"

Michelle answered, "Sure, Nora. How could I forget my wedding day?"

"The passenger dock you came through is right next to the freight docks. There's a corridor joining the two, though hardly anyone uses it any more. The freight dock runs the length of the station, so you can take it all the way down to the ship maintenance sector."

"That sounds perfect, Nora." Michelle pulled up HR on her station map. "I'm guessing the room labeled 'Orientation' is the one we want?"

"Yes. And just on the other side of that room you should see the corridor."

Michelle scrolled around the screen, zoomed in, and grinned. "Got it."

"Good girl. Now, if any of my HR people or any of those freight handlers try to stop you, just wave that pad around and tell them you've got your orders."

"That's what Matt and I did earlier this evening. Look like you belong, act preoccupied with work, and most people leave you alone. Daddy taught me that trick years ago."

And that's exactly what Michelle and I did. She held the pad in the crook of her arm and referred to it anytime someone from HR came near. We got the occasional nod you get when you pass people in a hallway, but even those were rare. Once again, the coveralls rendered us all but invisible.

Moments later, we walked through the orientation room and the door toward the passenger dock. The door to the freight docks was right where the map showed it. I waved my ID chip before the reader and the door slid aside. When we opened the door at the far end of the corridor, the noise came as a shock after the quiet of HR after hours.

Shouts echoed through the vast chamber, machinery whined and whirred, and gears ground together. Freight handlers and lift trucks and even a few men wearing heavy duty exoskeletons streamed past us toward the outer skin of the station. I glanced in that direction.

"It looks like a big cargo ship just docked." I pointed to our right. "I'd expected this place to be pretty quiet at this time of night."

"It's always busy in the freight docks, Matt," Greg said into the comm. "And you ought to be glad of it, since that's how your family started building their fortune."

"Busy is good for us," Michelle added. "If everyone has something to do, they won't have time to pay attention to a couple of maintenance techs. Let's go, Matt."

Michelle and I headed out, moving straight across all the freight handlers. We found ourselves dodging men and machines and men wearing machines so frequently our progress slowed to a crawl.

Halfway across the docking bay, Greg's urgent voice intruded on our concentration. "Kids, I just noticed Cummings' ID signal is closing in on that docking bay. He'll be there in less than a minute."

"Do you think he knows we're in here?" I asked.

"I can't see how, Matt. Your signal is still bouncing all over the entertainment sector. Besides, if he knew where you were, he'd bring his whole crew. It's just him and Spitz coming your way."

Michelle bit her lip. "Then why is he coming here?"

A thought came to me—one I did not like at all. I snatched the pad from Michelle and tapped the shoulder of a man passing in front of us. "I'm sorry to bother you, but is this the ship from Hippogriff Hauling?"

The man looked at me. "Hippogriff? Never heard of them. This here is an ore hauler from Redshift Mining."

I groaned loudly and turned to Michelle. "See? I *told* you this was the wrong ship. Now we're going to be late." Turning back to the man, I added, "Thanks. Gotta run."

Grabbing Michelle's arm, I dragged her around behind the man, who shrugged and resumed walking toward the freighter.

"Damn, damn, dammit!"

"Don't overreact, Matt." Michelle peeled my hand off her arm. "We're still swallowed up in a huge crowd."

"Do either of you two want to let Nora and me in on the problem?"

"Sorry, Greg. Redshift Mining is Hector's company."

"Hector? The man whose son attacked you?"

"The same. And he wants me dead in the worst way."

"Slow down, Matt." Michelle caught my belt and pulled back on it. "You're less noticeable if you walk at a normal pace. Besides, it's possible Hector isn't even on that ship."

"Why else would Cummings come to this docking bay?" I wanted to break into a run but followed Michelle's suggestion. "It's certain he sent word to Hector that he'd found us. If you were Hector, wouldn't you be on the next ship?"

Michelle sighed. "Yes, I'm sure you're right. But surely Hector will also wait for Cummings before going anywhere. And he'll wait at the ship, which is over two hundred meters away from us. Just relax."

I took a deep breath and let it out. "You're right. Sorry."

Michelle smiled brightly. "I know you're anxious and nervous and excited right now. Just try to keep everything in perspective."

And for two whole minutes I did keep everything in perspective. Then we passed in front of a slow moving man wearing an exoskeleton. We glanced up before crossing to make sure we wouldn't get in his way.

"I've finally found you, *bitch*!"

The man driving the exoskeleton was Crane, the freight handler Michelle took down in orientation. A feral grin spread across the man's face as he lifted his right arm. Servos whined and the right freight-handling arm rose as well. With a sweep, he brought the exoskeleton's arm down and around at Michelle and me. I reached out to grab Michelle and jump out of the way, but she beat me to it. Michelle's shoulder drove into my chest and we fell away from the descending steel arm.

Around us, workers yelled and scrambled away from Crane. The exoskeleton towered over us, the left arm now raised. With an incoherent roar, Crane clumped forward and tried to smash us. Still holding onto Michelle, I rolled desperately toward the scattering crowd. The whole docking bay rang as the arm clanged into the deck mere centimeters behind us.

We clambered to our feet as Crane fought to bring the two arms back into position for an attack. With servos calibrated for the deliberate movement required to move freight, the exoskeleton wasn't designed for fighting. Still, Crane only had to hit Michelle once and his wild gyrations showed he didn't care who he knocked out of the way to get her.

"Can you distract him for a few seconds?" I asked as we backpedaled from Crane. "I've got an idea, but I have to get in close."

"Go for it."

Michelle dove, tucked, and rolled away from me. As I expected, Crane's eyes tracked her. Against all my instincts to protect my wife, I ran in the opposite direction. Coming out of her roll, Michelle darted in toward Crane, keeping his attention riveted on her. Circling behind Crane, I ran at his back.

"That's enough of that, Crane!" a voice cracked from behind me. "Stop this nonsense now."

Crane looked over his shoulder at the speaker and caught sight of me closing in. Crane's right arm, raised to attack Michelle, swung down at me. Diving to the deck, I rolled into Crane's swing. The arm passed over me, no more than a hand's width away. Sparks flew as the arm scraped along the deck after it missed me. I wasted no time, bounding to my feet and then springing onto the exoskeleton frame.

Spittle flew from Crane's mouth as he snarled, "Stupid move, boy. Now I can get you without this suit."

Crane pulled his hand from the glove controlling the right

hand and started withdrawing his arm from the servo control rings. Grabbing a support bar, I swung behind Crane.

"Hiding behind me won't help you none once I'm free."

"Who said I was hiding?"

I let the stun stick drop out of my sleeve. Grabbing the collar of Crane's control suit, I stretched it out from his neck. I thumbed on the stun stick and jammed it down the back of the control suit. A single swipe of a stun stick causes searing pain and brief paralysis. Crane had a stick in constant contact with his back. Pain ripped through him and his muscles locked, bringing his exoskeleton to a stop.

Ignoring Crane's roar of agony, I jumped down and ran to Michelle. "Are you okay?"

Eyes shining with the excitement and adrenaline surging through her system, she nodded and pulled me in for a quick kiss. "That was a good idea, Matt."

Greg's voice shattered our moment. "Your little ruckus attracted a lot of attention. Several calls were placed to security. Worse, Cummings is in the docking bay and closing in on your position."

"Hey, are you two okay?" It was the man who had shouted at Crane. "I had one of my guys call security. They ought to be here soon." The man hooked a thumb at Crane. "What did you do to my moron freight guy? Not that he didn't deserve whatever you did."

"I shoved a stun stick down his back."

Surprise lit the man's face. "Since when do they let maintenance techs carry those?"

Michelle broke in and ignored the question. "I'm sorry, but we have to leave. We've got an emergency job."

Michelle grabbed my arm and pulled me away. The man grabbed my other arm and held me in place.

"I don't think so, lady. You don't just walk away from something like this."

Looking past the man holding my arm, I saw Cummings

dodging through the crowd, Spitz right on his heels. Both of them peered through the crowd every chance they got, but I had no idea if they'd seen us yet.

I pried the man's fingers from my arm. "You want answers, call HR and ask for Nora Ospin. She'll answer all your questions. But now we have to go."

This time, the man let me walk away.

"We've got to get lost in the crowd *fast*, Michelle. I just saw Cummings."

As if on cue, Cummings shouted, "Stop those two maintenance techs! They stole valuable equipment from my ship."

Heads swung from Cummings to us. As much as we hated playing to Cummings' story, we broke into a run. A hand clutched at me in a half-hearted manner, then another. Ahead of me, Michelle pulled her stun stick from her sleeve and swiped it in an arc in front of her. People fell away from the stick and a path cleared before us.

Taking a cue from Cummings' ploy, I shouted, "She's got the stun stick because the ship guy is stalking her. You can't let him get his hands on her."

Whether from my story or the stun stick, a path through the crowd opened before us and we sprinted through it. Looking over my shoulder, I saw the path closing up behind us.

"Move! Let me through! I've got to catch those thieves!" Cummings and Spitz fought to follow us as the wall of humanity closed around them.

Seconds later, we broke through the outer edge of the crowd. Still running, we dodged in and out of the fringes of the workers heading to unload the ore carrier.

Greg's voice came in from the comm. "Nice work with the cover stories. Nora's on the comm with that foreman you talked to. She's asked the crowd to hold Cummings and Spitz until security gets there. You should be home free."

We dodged around a few more people and broke out into the open.

A harsh, familiar voice sounded from our right. "Yeah, that's them, all right. Two year's salary for each of you when you catch them."

Hector stood ten meters away from us—and he'd brought at least a dozen of his crewmen. Without exchanging a word, Michelle and I turned and ran along the edge of the crowd.

"Go get 'em, men!"

Hector's command galvanized his crew to action. They sprinted after us, spreading out in the hopes of hemming us in.

"Greg? We need help. Hector did come with his ship and just he sicced a dozen of his men on us." I risked a glance over my shoulder. "We're holding even with them right now, but I don't know how long we can keep it up."

"How close are they?" Greg responded.

"Maybe ten meters."

"Okay, so you don't have time to wait for a door to open. I'm checking the map for- Hey!"

"Matt? Michelle?" Nora's voice replaced Greg's. "Sorry to grab the comm from Greg, but I know what to do. How far are you from the crowd of dock workers?"

"Thirty meters or so," Michelle answered. "We've been avoiding them because dodging through the crowd will slow us down."

"Run toward them right now. I suppose you're still wearing that shapeless coverall, Michelle?"

"Of course. It's supposed to be my disguise."

"There's nothing we can do about that, now," Nora said. "But you can take off the hat and let that blond hair of yours fall free."

Michelle looked as confused as I did, but she pulled off the cap and her long hair tumbled out. "She's taken off the hat, Nora. Can you please explain what that does for us?"

"Matt, start shouting that the men behind you are after your wife. Claim they're in league with Cummings and made a deal to buy her. Shout whatever you can think of along those lines. And

Michelle, I'm sure it goes against the grain, but a little screaming and crying on your part will help sell this."

I wasted no time following Nora's suggestion. "Help us! Somebody help! They're from that ship and they want to take my wife!"

A few heads turned our way, just in time for Michelle's scream, "Please! Oh God, don't let them get me!"

More heads turned and a few men turned and lumbered in our direction. Behind us, it appeared Hector's men hadn't heard our cries for help. More freight workers pointed and came to our aid. The first one to reach us, a hulk of a man, said, "You get that girl outta here, son. We got yer back."

"Thank you so much!" Michelle cried to the men as we ran past them.

Behind us, the hulking man's voice rang out, "That's far enough, ship scum. We don't take kindly to yer kind terrorizing our women."

One of Hector's men replied in kind. "This ain't none of yer business, baggage boy."

With an angry roar, the freight workers attacked and Hector's men went down under a pile of massive men.

"Great idea, Nora. That worked like a charm. If there's a video feed of that, identify as many of those men as possible. I'm going to reward them when this is over."

"I'm glad I could help, Matt. But I suggest you and Michelle get out of the docking bay now. Hector is still out there and we don't know how many men he has available. I'm giving the comm back to Greg, now."

A second later, Greg spoke. "I agree with Nora's assessment. While she talked to you, I found the closest exit out of the docking bay."

Michelle donned her cap and tucked her hair up under it. "Just point us in the right direction, Greg."

"Head directly away from the docked ship. The far wall has a hatch into the entertainment sector. Turn right and the warehouse sector is less than fifty meters away."

Michelle caught my arm and led off toward the door. "How about Hector? Can you setup a trace on him?"

"No, lass, I can't. Hector isn't from Pegasus Station and won't have an implant." Greg's voice grew thoughtful. "Then again, if Hector is mixed up with Cummings, he might also be involved in holding Matt's parents. He might have a chip that isn't part of the official record."

Michelle glanced at me. "Say he has a chip. Have you got any idea how to find it, Matt?"

"Maybe. It depends on Greg's skills."

"Then you're in luck, lad," Greg exclaimed. "I'm as good as they get. On Pegasus Station, anyway. What's your idea?"

"Is the other trace process running? The one tracking Michelle and me?"

"Yep, it's still chugging away even though it can't be of any use with your IDs hopping all over the sector."

"Whoever setup that process works with Cummings or for him. It's possible that hacker knows about stuff like unofficial ID chips. I mean, someone has to handle the database stuff." Michelle and I reached the door in the far wall. The silence beyond that door was almost deafening. "So, if you can find out who's controlling that process..."

"Now, why didn't I think of that?" I heard Greg tapping enthusiastically on the pad. "Well, that was just too easy. Our hacker obviously thinks no one besides him will ever get this level of access."

"You know who it is?"

"Yep. So do you, Matt." Greg sighed. "It's your friend and co-worker John."

Joking, good-natured John? Seeing Michelle's quizzical look, I said, "He's the one member of the team who's sort of close to my own age. Greg, isn't John too young to be involved in this?"

"Not really. He started when he was about your age. Nora can check his start date, but I'm pretty sure it was a month or so before your parents disappeared."

Nora called from somewhere away from the comm. "Greg's got a good memory. You know, as HR director I can tell security we've had complaints and have him brought to me."

"Have Nora do it," Michelle told Greg. "But I can tell you a really simple way to find out just how deeply John is involved."

I raised my eyebrows. "Do tell, my dear, because I've got nothing."

"Greg, check the permissions assigned to John's ID chip." Michelle flashed a smug grin at me. "If he's got the same special clearance Cummings has, we know he's in deep."

"That's a clever girl you married, Matt."

"She married me—of course she's clever."

Greg snorted and Michelle jabbed my side playfully. Then Greg sighed. "He's got the permission, Matt. If he's in that deep, I don't know if we can sweat anything useful out of him. We're going to try, though. Nora says he'll be here in a few minutes."

Michelle and I left the entertainment sector behind and entered the warehouse sector. With a big ore carrier in dock, the place bustled with activity. Michelle and I just sauntered along, minding our own business and checking our pad every few minutes. Like last time, no one gave us a second glance.

Then we rounded a corner and, thirty meters ahead of us, saw Hector standing in the middle of an intersection and staring right at us. Worse, he wore a blaster at his hip.

BEHIND THE DOOR

A couple of warehouse workers stood between Hector and me, chatting just outside an overhead door. The one facing Hector noticed his intense stare down the corridor and glanced over his shoulder. I guess I looked just as intense because the guy grabbed his friend's arm and started hurrying toward Hector and the intersection.

In that instant I got sick and tired of this whole melodrama—tired of running, tired of laying low, tired of sneaking, and truly sick and tired of Hector and Cummings. I threw my arms wide and yelled, "Here I am, Hector. Are you here to shoot me? Huh? Is that it?"

"Matt, what are you doing?" Michelle grabbed my left arm and tried to drag me back the way we'd come.

I pulled my arm free and stalked toward Hector. "I'm not running from this guy again, Michelle." I raised my voice, "Did you hear that, Hector? I'm not running. You want to shoot me, here's your chance."

Hector stared at me, his blaster still holstered and surprise written across his face.

"Why aren't you shooting, Hector? Is it because you've seen the vids of the shootout on Rockville Station? Is it because you know Paco ambushed us and *still* couldn't kill either one of us?" My voice took on a taunting edge and I didn't care. "You're not shooting because you're scared you'll end up in prison. Aren't you? Huh?"

Michelle caught hold of the back of my coverall and tried to pull me back. "Stop taunting him before he really *does* kill you."

I stopped walking, only three meters between Hector and me. Hector's hands clenched and unclenched, his face white with rage.

"Screw the blaster, Hector. You know what you really want to do is beat me to a pulp." I raised my chin and tapped my jaw. "What do you say, rock jock? Give me your best shot. Come on!"

"Yeah, I will. I'm gonna beat you to death, boy." Hector balled his fists and raised them into a proper boxing stance. His gaze locked on my jaw and his eyes gleaming with anticipation, Hector took a step toward me.

I pulled the taser from my pocket and shot him. Hector's eyes widened, then the dart hit him in the chest. He convulsed once and then collapsed to the ground.

Pocketing the taser, I turned around and grinned at Michelle. Her fist hit me square under the jaw. "Don't you *ever* do something like that again! God, Matt, I thought you'd lost your mind."

"Ouch." I rubbed my jaw. "I'm sorry, Michelle. I just snapped. When I realized it was working—that Hector wasn't shooting me —I ran with it. I'd have told you if I could."

"Idiot." Michelle bent over her pad, scrolling around the sector map. "You took Hector out, hero, you get to carry him."

"Let's just leave him where he is."

"So he can chase after us when he recovers from the shock?" Michelle pointed down a side corridor. "No thank you."

"You mean he won't be out for hours?"

"Try five minutes, Matt. GenCo makes tasers, why don't you know that?"

I groaned lifting Hector and throwing him over my shoulder. Staggering after Michelle, I said, "Tasers never interested me. Uh, where are we taking him?"

"There's a security door down here—high level access is required to open it from either side." Michelle flashed a predatory smile over her shoulder. "Unless Hector has an ID chip we don't know about, he'll be trapped."

"Who will be trapped?" Greg's voice sounded from the comm.

"Weren't you listening, Greg?"

"Sorry, had to slip out for a minute. Security just brought John to HR and Nora wanted to try putting the fear of God in him before he saw me, too."

I filled Greg in as Michelle waved her hand before a reader. The security door beside it slid open. I dropped Hector inside the door and took his blaster. Michelle shut the door and we started back to the main corridor.

"Did that work? Is John talking?" Michelle asked.

"Not quite yet, but Nora's working him over good. Oh, she just waved me in. I'm muting the comm but can still hear you." With a click, the comm went silent.

"Do you think they're going to get anything from him?" Michelle asked as we resumed our walk toward ship maintenance.

"Maybe. I think John is good at hacking computers, but he's no criminal mastermind."

We walked in silence for a while before Michelle spoke again. "So, stun or kill?"

"Huh?"

"Hector's blaster. Is it set to stun or kill?" Michelle affected a casual tone, but I detected plenty of underlying tension.

I looked behind us and, seeing we were alone in the corridor, pulled out the blaster. "Let's see... It's set to kill."

"Apparently God *still* watches out for fools—that's good to know." Michelle held out her hand. "Give. I'm a better shot than you."

"True." I put the gun in her hand. "You ought to give me the stun stick, then."

Michelle nodded, let the stick drop out of her sleeve, and offered it to me stun end first.

"It *is* turned off, isn't it?" I smiled, taking the stick without waiting for an answer.

Five minutes later, we crossed into ship maintenance. My heart beat faster. A few more minutes and we would stand before the door. What, besides my parents, lay beyond it?

"Greg, this is Matt." I spoke into the comm. "We're in ship maintenance now. The door is nearby. If you've got anything for us, share it now."

The comm clicked and we heard sounds from Nora's office. "John claims he doesn't know much. He says he gave himself the extra permission because he could, but he doesn't know what it does."

"Do you and Nora believe him?" Michelle asked.

Greg sighed, "Yeah, we do. John's one of those stupid smart kids. You know the type."

Michelle turned a brief glare on me. "Far too well."

"He's in way over his head. He gets his orders from Cummings and the system traffic control manager, Arthur Jewel. We're checking on him, now," Greg said. In the background, I heard Nora say something to Greg. "Hang on, Nora wants the comm."

Nora's voice came on. "I think we've got everything we're going to get from John, but he did have one last interesting bit of information. There's someone else involved in this who isn't from Pegasus Station. John has no idea who the person is, just that they have every permission imaginable, including a couple John can't trace."

"You figure that's the person in charge?" I asked.

"Either that or they report to the person in charge. The thing is, John thinks that person is on station right now." Nora took a deep breath. "Matt, I know you're afraid something bad will happen if we call security, and you may be right. But once you go through that door, I'm giving you thirty minutes to come back out then I'm calling security."

I opened my mouth to protest but Michelle spoke faster. "I

agree with Nora. If we can't get in and out in that time, we're going to need some serious help."

I closed my mouth and nodded. Then we rounded a corner and stood before the door. I waved my hand across the reader. With a soft whoosh, the door slid open.

"Nora, start your timer," Michelle said. "We're going in."

Michelle and I stepped through the door and into...a simple storage area. The room was maybe five meters wide and seven deep, with crates stacked against the right and left walls. A few more crates were scattered in the middle of the floor. And that was it.

Michelle poked me in the back. "Don't just stand in the doorway, Matt. Go in so I can shut the door."

I did as she asked and heard the door quietly whoosh shut behind me. My face obviously gave my thoughts away. Michelle came around in front of me and took my hands in hers.

"Nora's timer is running, babe. If you don't want station security crashing our party before it begins, we've got to get started." She released one hand and turned, letting her gaze sweep the room. "I wonder where it is."

"Where *what* is?" Annoyance or despair—maybe both—crept into my voice. "There's nothing here, Michelle."

"Were you expecting a big, blinking arrow saying '*This way to Matt's parents*'?" Michelle let go of my hand and walked to the back wall. "Cummings and Morgan spent hours behind this door and I doubt they whiled away the time stacking boxes. Look for hidden controls or doors or both."

Michelle ran her hands over the back wall, staring at it from different angles. After a few seconds, she looked over her shoulder at me. "It's a big room, Matt, I could use some help with this."

I gave myself a shake and joined my wife at the back wall. "You've got more training in this stuff than me, Michelle. What should I look for?"

"Minor differences in coloration, narrow lines indicating seams, fingertip-sized shiny spots, that sort of thing. Check everything from multiple angles. Differences in reflection show up better that way." She continued running her hands over the wall while instructing me. "You might pick up a seam by touch, too."

I mimicked her techniques. "What about the crates. Could what we're looking for be inside one of them?"

"It's possible, but if anyone unauthorized ever did get in here— a thief or customs inspector, say—they'd check the boxes and ignore the walls."

"All right, that makes-"

With a gentle jerk, the room began moving down.

"What did you do?" Michelle and I both said to each other.

Our gazes locked for a second. Michelle recovered first. "We've got to hide!"

"Check the crates." I ran to the closest one. "Maybe some of them are empty."

The few crates scattered around the floor had packing material up to their lids. I hopped on the row of boxes to the right and Michelle took the ones to the left. How long did we have before the room stopped moving? My parental pointings never really pointed down, so it couldn't be long. I threw open the lid to the first crate. Packing material again.

"I've got an empty one over here, Matt."

I leapt down and dashed across the room as Michelle climbed into the crate. I bounded up and climbed in next to her. The fit was tight but I knew we'd manage. I squatted, pulling the lid down on top of us. Just after the lid closed over us, the room stopped moving.

Seconds later, footsteps echoed in the small room. Whoever was out there walked across to the wall we'd been examining. A click sounded. A few seconds later the room started up. Another click sounded, then the footsteps headed back toward the door.

Suddenly, Michelle stood and threw back the crate's lid. I hastily stood next to her. An extremely surprised, muscular man in his late thirties stared at us. More accurately, he stared at the blaster Michelle aimed at him.

"Federation Bureau of Investigation, Mr. Morgan." The blaster and her businesslike tone sold her bluff far better than her appearance did. "Down on the floor. *Now!*"

Morgan crowded closer to the door. With the room still moving up, I don't know what he hoped to accomplish with that. Michelle moved her aim slightly and fired. The blaster bolt scorched the floor between Morgan's feet.

"The next one burns your leg, Mr. Morgan."

Eyes bugging out, Morgan dropped to the floor.

"Agent Atwood, restrain the prisoner."

I climbed out of the crate, careful not to jostle Michelle or get in her line of fire. Jumping to the floor, I removed the belt to my coveralls and pulled out the stun stick. Waving the stick before Morgan's eyes, I circled behind him. "If you try anything, Morgan, I'll ram this stick down your pants and leave it on until its charge drains out. Now, put your hands behind your back."

With another gentle jerk, the room finished its ascent. I tucked the stun stick under my arm and wrapped the belt around Morgan's right wrist. With considerable strength, Morgan pulled his right arm over his head, jerking me off balance. The stun stick fell to the floor as I tottered. Morgan rolled over and kicked me in the chest. He grabbed the stun stick as I fell backward. Staying on the floor, Morgan jabbed the now-humming stun stick at me.

Crack! Crack! Morgan writhed as two blaster shots hit him in the back. The stun stick rolled from his grasp and I kicked it across the room. With a sigh of escaping breath, Morgan settled onto the floor.

"Are you okay, Matt?" Michelle still stood in the crate, the blaster trained on the still form of Morgan.

"Yeah, I'm fine." I fetched the stun stick, never taking my eye from Morgan.

Keeping the blaster ready, Michelle climbed one-handed from the crate. "Can you help me down, honey?"

I lifted Michelle down and together we approached Morgan. Keying the stun stick on, I touched Morgan's leg. It jerked, but nothing else happened. Cautiously, I checked his throat for a pulse, finding nothing.

"I think he's dead, Michelle."

"Okay." Michelle pocketed the blaster and returned to the back wall.

"How are you doing? I mean, I know what shooting Paco did to me."

"I'm okay to keep going, if that's what you mean." Michelle began pushing spots all around the back wall. "I'll let it bother me once this is over."

A click sounded beneath Michelle's fingers and a small panel popped open in the back wall. She pulled it open, revealing a button and another chip reader.

"Before we do anything else, shouldn't we hide Morgan's body?" I asked.

Michelle nodded and we spent the next several minutes wrestling the body into the empty crate. Then Michelle returned to studying the panel.

"Why don't you push the button?"

Michelle sighed. "We've got two controls. I don't know whether we use both in a particular order or if one is a decoy. Either way, I bet doing it wrong sets off an alarm somewhere."

I joined her, studying the panel. "I bet it's the chip reader then the button. Or just the chip reader. But the chip reader should be first because it tells the system you're authorized to use it."

"That makes as much sense as anything." Michelle waved her hand before the reader. Nothing happened. She pressed the button.

With a gentle jerk, the room began descending.

A BIG SURPRISE

I stared at the door, trying to imagine what I'd see when it opened. Maybe a small apartment with an attached workshop so Dad could work for his captors? Maybe prison cells and a torture chamber?

Michelle pressed up against the wall to the left of the door. She pointed to the space on the other side of the door. "We don't know what we're going to find down there, Matt, so get out of sight."

With a nod, I abandoned my speculation and mirrored her position. Michelle drew her blaster, holding it up and ready. I did the same with my taser.

"The first thing we do when the door opens is lean back from the wall and take a look." Michelle's intense gaze caught my eyes. "Don't put your head in front of the opening until we've seen what we can from both angles. Okay?"

"Got it."

The room stopped moving. With a gentle whoosh, the door slid open, letting in unexpected sounds and smells. Men called to one another, the echoes indicating a vast open area. Machinery thrummed and whined and hammered. The odor of lubrication and fuel and ozone tingled in our noses.

"What the hell?" I whispered, leaning toward the door to find out what lay beyond.

"Matt," Michelle hissed. "Remember what I said?"

With chagrin, I nodded and leaned back from the wall. The angle cut off two thirds of the view through the door and what little I could see wasn't interesting. "I've got a wall two meters to the left of the door. What about you?"

"I've got...a lot more than that." Michelle blinked wide eyes a couple of times. "I think it's safe to risk a short look out of the door."

I looked through the door and immediately understood Michelle's reaction. The chamber beyond the door was huge, at least three hundred meters long and another hundred meters deep. Our door was tucked into a dark corner, accessible by a catwalk. Hundreds of men swarmed on the floor far below us. Machinery of all shapes and sizes lined the walls, with more rolled out into position on the floor.

All of this activity centered on two large spaceships nestled in docks. At first glance, both ships were simple freighters. But the engines, their shielding removed for maintenance, belonged on a military cruiser, not a heavy, wallowing freighter. And all along the sides of both ships, sections of the hull lay open. Heavy ship lasers and missile launchers extended through the camouflaged weapon ports.

Michelle caught my arm and pulled me through the door and onto the catwalk. "We've got to shut the door. The light from the room will catch someone's attention, if we don't."

Once on the catwalk, Michelle waved her hand before the chip reader. The door shut and shadowed darkness settled over us. Michelle crouched, peering through the railing, and I followed her example.

"You're the one who knows about spaceships, Matt. Can you tell me what we're looking at?"

"Q-ships," I answered absently, still staring at the scene below.

"Thanks, honey. Please try again, and this time speak in a language I comprehend."

"Right. Sorry, I'm just..." I waved a hand toward the scene below. "I didn't expect anything like this."

"Yeah, me neither." Michelle caught my chin and turned my head to face her. "What are Q-ships?"

"In simple terms, they're warships disguised as freighters. Although in this case, I'd bet they're pirate ships disguised as freighters."

"That explains a lot. Your parents must have discovered this operation and then the pirates grabbed them to keep them quiet." Michelle bit her lip. "But that doesn't explain why they kept your parents alive. And how did a bunch of pirates manage to build this inside such a huge space station?"

I shook my head. "You've got the chronology wrong. The space station was built around this place. Unless I miss my guess, you're looking at the original Pegasus Station. Over the last century, the rest of the station was built around it and this place was abandoned. Or so everyone thinks."

"Matt, you know this couldn't have been done without help from high ranking people inside GenCo."

"I know. I suppose those stories about the GenCo fortune being built on pirate loot are true, after all." I rested my forehead on the catwalk railing. "You know, finding out you're the great grandson of a pirate isn't as romantic as I thought it would be."

Michelle's hand rubbed my back gently. "You haven't done anything wrong, Matt."

"You mean besides living a life of luxury bought with blood money?"

"Let's save recriminations for later—like after we have your parents and know the full story." Michelle scooted closer to me. "Right now, let's figure out exactly where your parents are."

"I don't think I can, Michelle. My mind is swirling too much to-"

Michelle interrupted me with a kiss—as deep, loving, and lusty a kiss as she'd ever laid on me. You might think I'd be used to these kisses by now. I'm not and hope I never will be. The swirling in my mind slowed, then stopped, leaving my psychic power free to do it's work. Michelle blazed like a beacon. My parents shone like a bright light in the darkness. And a fourth, dimmer light flickered to life for a few seconds before vanishing. Someone down on the floor must have had a very brief, very intense emotion.

Michelle finished the kiss and pulled back. We both followed my pointing arm. On the far side of the docking bay, stuck in a darkened corner similar to ours, lights burned behind three windows.

"It looks like some kind of apartment or something. Maybe the old station offices?" Michelle offered.

"It doesn't matter. That's where we need to go. If we're lucky, the catwalk goes all the way around."

To the right, the catwalk ended after twenty meters, with metal stairs zigzagging down to the docking bay floor. So Michelle and I went in the other direction. With the darkness and shadows, we couldn't tell if the walk ended after thirty meters or ran on for three hundred.

"Can you tell what they're doing with the ships?" Michelle asked.

"It looks like they're prepping the ships to go hunting."

"That must be where the guy in traffic control comes in," Michelle mused. "With a little creative routing, he can give these ships the chance to slip out of their docks without anyone noticing where they came from."

"That's how I'd do it if I was in charge."

"Which brings up the question of who is in charge." Michelle stopped and turned back to me. "If this started with your family, why didn't your father know about it? Why wasn't he running it?"

"Maybe they figured Dad was too honest to keep the family business alive. Or my grandfather was. Or my great grandfather didn't want his children involved in piracy." I shrugged, frustrated at how little we knew. "Or maybe someone outside of the family took over running the operation. I mean, GenCo earns far more in one day than the pirates' probably take in a year. It doesn't make any financial sense for someone in the family to be involved."

"At one time it made sense for your family—and today it makes a lot of sense for Cummings and Hector." Michelle started along the catwalk again. "I guess we'll find out when this all comes out."

Straight ahead of us, a voice rang out. "Move it about a meter to the left. Almost. Yes, there. Now, get it bolted in place."

Someone else was on the catwalk with us. The echoes of the man's shout faded quickly into the cacophony of sounds in the docking bay. Michelle and I crouched on the catwalk, both of us straining to see into the deep shadows enveloping the upper reaches of the docking bay.

"Can you see the guy?" I whispered.

"Not yet," Michelle hissed back. "Keep watching. If he shouts again, the sound might help us find him in the shadows."

I did as Michelle instructed. About ten seconds later the man shouted more instructions to his crew below. Ready for it this time, I spotted the man. "Got him. He's about fifteen meters ahead, leaning on the railing. Look to the right of the middle lighted window in the office where my parents are being held."

"I see him, now." Michelle stared at the man, biting her lip. "We can't afford to wait for him to finish and walk away—not with Nora planning on calling station security in twenty minutes. This whole setup is way bigger than either of us imagined and completely beyond the capabilities of the security team."

"Maybe the Feds' response to my DNA scan will be big enough to tackle these pirates, but we still have to get my parents out of harm's way before this all goes down."

"We will, Matt." Michelle reached over and squeezed my hand. "But first, let's get past that guy on the catwalk."

"It's really loud in here. I bet we can get close enough for me to shoot him with my taser."

"We'll make a *real* security guy out of you, yet." Michelle grinned and started creeping toward our target.

To my ears, the catwalk creaked and groaned with every step we took. I was sure the man couldn't help but hear us coming—except he didn't. He kept his attention on the work going on below, shouting instructions every now and then. I held my taser ready to fire when we got to within half a dozen meters of the man. With my next step, the catwalk gave a sharp creak. The man turned idly our way and his eyes bugged out when he spotted Michelle and me.

He straightened in shock at the same moment I fired my taser. I fired a second shot, just to be sure I got the man. The first dart caught him center mass, just above his heart. The man convulsed from the jolt, falling against the catwalk railing. Balanced precariously, he clutched at the top rail just as the second dart caught him in the right shoulder. The man's arm straightened involuntarily as the charge shot through it and his hand missed its grip. With horror shining in his eyes, the man overbalanced and toppled over the rail!

We were too far from the man to do anything to help him. As he tumbled from sight, Michelle caught my hand and dragged me forward into a run.

"Come on! Our countdown timer just got a whole lot shorter."

Abandoning all of our attempts at stealth, we pounded along the catwalk as fast as we could run. I listened for the sound of the man hitting the deck after his hundred meter fall, but never heard a thing. I *did* hear shouts erupt from far below, dashing my hope the man had landed unnoticed and in deep shadows.

Suddenly, I caught a glimpse of an out-of-place junction box at the end of a short branch off of the main catwalk. I pulled up, dragging Michelle to a stop, too.

"Hang on, I need to check this out."

"We don't have time for this, Matt. Unless the pirates are idiots, this whole catwalk will be swarming with them in a few minutes."

"We're making time, Michelle." I dragged her over to the junction box. "I can't see a reason for this to be here unless it has something to do with the shields that protect this place from scanners and comms."

Michelle stopped trying to drag me back to the main catwalk. "Can you turn it off from this box?"

"I doubt it, but maybe I can short it out." I opened the box, pulled out my pocket light, and shined it around the inside.

"Matt, hurry. That light will give us away to anyone who gets within fifty meters of us."

"I know, babe, but reminding me isn't helpful." I flicked the light over relays and connectors, then tugged and pulled at those to see what lay hidden behind them. "Ah ha! Just as I thought."

As I checked my tools for a vibroblade, Michelle looked over my shoulder at the box. "What do you see?"

"A computerized control unit. Something as complex as the shield requires precise balancing or seams open up in the shield." Grinning, I pulled out the utility knife I'd been looking for. "Each junction box has to have its own controller to keep the shield up."

Flicking on the blade, I jammed it straight into the control unit. The unit gave a soft pop and a small curl of smoke rose from it. Thumbing off both the light and the blade, I closed the junction box.

"Did that even do anything?" Michelle asked.

"Let's find out." I thumbed my comm unit on. "Greg? Are you there?"

"Nora! It's Matt on the comm." Relief filled Greg's voice. "Have you got your parents? Are you out of there?"

"No to both, Greg." As she spoke, Michelle grabbed my hand and we ran back to the main catwalk. "Things are a lot more complicated than we thought they were."

With the same economy of words she'd displayed reporting to Jonas back on Draconis, Michelle told Greg what we had discovered. "Right now, we could use some serious help. The pirates are coming up to the catwalk to find out who killed their man. We're close to Matt's parents, but I don't know what we're going to find there or how we'll get out again once we get there."

"Roger that, Michelle. Nora is calling the security chief now. What do you need me to do?"

Michelle shot a glance at me. "Matt, have you got any ideas?"

"Call Nancy Martin, the flight commander. Bring her up to speed and get her fighter wing out on patrol. I don't know how much good it'll do, but it can't hurt."

"I'll get right on it," Greg said. "As for you— Hey, who are you?"

Dull thumps came over the comm. It sounded like someone grabbed the comm from Greg.

Panic welled up inside me. Were Greg and Nora in danger because they helped us? "Greg? Are you okay?"

"Greg is fine, sir. I didn't want to waste time with explanations."

"Daddy!" Michelle cried.

"Jonas? How the hell did you get here so fast?" I asked.

"I'll explain later, sir." Jonas steady voice had a calming effect on both of us. "What's your situation?"

"The original Pegasus Station is now a base for pirates," Michelle answered. "They've got two of what Matt calls Q-ships. Those are-"

"I know what they are, pumpkin. Continue."

"The pirates outnumber us at least three hundred to one. They're about to block the only exit we know of. And we're about to break through a door and rescue Matt's parents. Then we need to get out of the pirate base, of course." Michelle took a deep breath. "And Matt and I got married."

Jonas was silent for a few seconds. "Let's get you two and Matt's parents out of the pirate base, first. Everything else can wait."

Over the comm, we heard Jonas ordering Greg to pull up station design diagrams. Far behind us, near the door into the elevator room, bright beams of light pierced the darkness as the pirates reached the catwalk. Dead ahead of us loomed the door into my parents...apartment? Prison?

A chip reader was installed beside the door. We pulled up and I waved my hand in front of the reader. With a click, the door slid open.

REUNION

I stepped inside, hoping to find my parents waiting for me. They weren't, at least not in the first room. We saw a few comp consoles with business pads next to them. A few desks even held paper records—easier to destroy quickly, I guess. All in all, the room looked like nothing more than the office for a typical small business. What would we find in those records? Did murderous, illegal small businesses have retirement funds or health insurance?

All of those thoughts flitted through my mind during the two seconds it took me to look around the office. Desperate to find my parents, I opened my mouth to call out to them. Michelle covered my mouth with her hand.

"Don't say anything. Your parents might be guarded," she whispered, waving her other hand before the chip reader on the inside. The door hissed shut behind us.

I nodded and Michelle withdrew her hand. Holding her blaster ready, she crept to the only other door in the room. To our surprise, it was an old fashioned door with a door knob and without any kind of chip reader. Michelle leveled the blaster on the door. I turned the knob and gently pushed the door open. We found a short hallway, three or four meters long and ending in another door.

We approached the second door with the same caution as the first and clearly heard sounds beyond it. Michelle leveled her blaster again. I turned the knob and gently pushed this door open. On the other side of the door lay a disconcertingly familiar sight—the room was identical to my parents' living room back on Draconis. A man and woman, their backs to us, sat in an exact copy of the love seat my parents always sat in. They watched a vid player identical to the one we'd had before they disappeared. I recognized the vid at once—*Star Ranger and the Slavers of Ursus*.

It was my absolute favorite vid seven years ago. I watched it so often Mom and Dad threatened to throw it in the recycler. I hadn't watch it once since their disappearance.

"Go away and leave us alone." The voice belonged to my father. It sounded older to me, less firm, but there was no doubt who was speaking. "This is our family time."

I tried to find my voice but couldn't. Seeing my mouth open and close, Michelle lowered her blaster and said, "Mr. and Mrs. Connaught, we're here to rescue you."

Two heads spun around and eyes widened in surprise. Mom found her voice first. "Mattie? Oh my God, is it you Mattie?"

The next thing I knew, I found myself leaning over the back of the love seat hugging my parents, with tears streaming down my cheeks. Mom covered my face in kisses while Dad just said, "Son!" and held me tight.

Behind me, Michelle spoke quietly to Jonas. I heard their conversation but had no idea what they said to each other. Mom, Dad, and I kept repeating the same inane things over and over again.

"We never thought we'd see you again!"

"I love you so much!"

"How did you find us?"

Then Michelle pulled me back from my parents. "I really hate to break up this reunion, but we've got work to do before you three can catch up with each other. The pirates will get here eventually and we need to be gone before then."

"Of course, you're right young lady. Who-" Dad sat back and took his first good look at Michelle. "Good God! Aren't you Jonas's little girl?"

"Yes sir. And I've got Daddy on this comm. I'm putting it on speaker so we can all hear him."

Michelle tapped a button on her comm and held it between us. "You're on, Daddy."

"Richard? Angela? Can you both hear me?"

"Loud and clear, Jonas," Dad said. "It's a relief to hear your voice. When this is over, you'll have to tell me how you found us."

"You'll have to ask our children. It's been all I can do to keep up with them." I detected definite pride in Jonas's voice. "But right now, let's concentrate on getting the four of you out of there."

"Have you got a plan, Jonas?" I asked.

"I think so, sir. Based on the station designs, it appears there's a huge door at one end of the original station. It keeps the pirate ships hidden until they go out raiding."

Mom and Dad both nodded, with Mom adding, "That's right. We can see the thing open and shut from here."

"Good. Your help—and your ride out of there—has to come through that door. Now comes the tough part. We can't find any way to control the door from here. Sir, can you hack the pirates' computer system and open the door?"

"I can try-"

Dad interrupted, "That won't work. The door can only be opened with a manual control. The pirates put it in place specifically to keep hackers from finding the door controls."

"Damn, that makes this a lot more complicated."

"No it doesn't, Daddy. It makes this a lot easier."

"No. Absolutely not. You are to stay put, young lady. With the pirates alerted to your presence, going out there is too dangerous."

"There aren't many places intruders can go down here, Daddy. Staying in one place is just as dangerous as going back out." Michelle frowned as if just thinking of something. "And you can drop that 'young lady' bit, too. I am a married woman, after all."

Mom and Dad exchanged surprised looks and then their eyes widened further. They turned toward me.

"I was going to tell you once we were all safe," I said. "And that's still the best time to talk about this."

"Jonas, did you approve their wedding? Is it part of your plan to keep Matt safe?" Mom asked.

"I learned about the marriage two minutes ago," Jonas replied. "But as much as I *want* to talk about it now, Matt is right. We'll discuss it once everyone is safe." Jonas paused for a few seconds. "All right, pump- um, Michelle, what's your plan?"

"I'm going to slip out of this little office-prison, sneak over to the controls, and open that big door. It'll be easy."

"No, it might not be that easy," I said. "What if there's a code on the door controls?"

"You can talk me through it from here, babe."

Mom's and Dad's eyebrows rose at Michelle's endearment as I shook my head. "It'll be easier if I'm there to do it myself. Besides, who will watch your back while I'm talking you through it?"

"No, it's too dangerous," Mom insisted. "Both of you are going to stay right here until help arrives."

"No, Mom, we're not. Michelle and I can handle this."

"Jonas?" Dad asked. "What do you think?"

"As Michelle's father and Matt's bodyguard and his...father-in-law, I think it's crazy dangerous." Jonas spoke slowly, as if working his way through complex feelings. "But from a strictly professional point of view, our kids are right. Someone has to open that door and they're the best ones to do it."

Silence hung over our little group when Jonas finished speaking. Then Dad said, "All right. But for God's sake, be careful."

Mom added, "Married couple or not, I'll ground you both for a year if you get yourselves killed."

Jonas, with help from Greg, told us where to find the door

controls. Of course, the controls were on the main floor of the docking bay.

My parents gave me quick, heartfelt hugs and surprised Michelle by hugging her, as well. Then the two of us went back to the door with the chip reader. Leaving the office's interior lights off, we slipped out and started toward the nearest set of stairs down from the catwalk.

I handed my comm unit to Michelle, replacing the one she'd left with my parents. "You keep this. Any advice Jonas offers will be for you, anyway."

Michelle fitted the comm into her ear. "Can everyone hear me? Good."

We reached the nearest set of stairs and, as silently as possible on old metal stairs, descended. The descent was surreal, though not for the reason you might think. While I found sneaking down to the ground floor of a pirate base disconcerting, I'd done equally disconcerting things since boarding the maglev train back on Draconis all those weeks ago. No, the surreality came from listening to Michelle's side of a three way conversation with my parents and her father. A conversation about us.

At first, she simply responded with a soft "Yes" or "No," leading me to believe the discussion centered around our current situation—and maybe that was the case. Then Michelle responded to a question obviously asked by my mother.

"I don't think any girl could study your son as closely as I have and not fall in love with him, ma'am."

"Michelle," I hissed, "tell my mother to save the third degree for when we aren't surrounded by pirates."

"It's all right, Matt. I can descend stairs and talk at the same time." Michelle listened for a few seconds then smiled. "Yes ma'am, that's pretty much exactly what Matt said."

We descended further as our parents continued questioning Michelle. "No, I don't think the marriage is premature. I love Matt and he loves me. And we both know it beyond all shadow of a doubt."

Michelle's eyes widened. "You figured that out, Daddy? I never did until he told me."

That almost made me miss a step. "Jonas figured out about my psychic ability?"

"Daddy says it took him years, but he spent more time around you than anyone. And he's really observant—it's part of what makes him so good at his job."

Her attention returned to the comm unit. "What's that, Daddy?" I almost missed it in the dim light, but suddenly Michelle blushed. "In, um, really...intimate...moments, Matt's feelings come through loud and clear...Well, if you don't want to hear the answers, then stop asking the questions, Daddy...Thank you, ma'am. I appreciate the support. And just in case anyone I call 'Daddy' is thinking of asking, I'll tell you right now that I am *not* pregnant."

By this time, we'd descended halfway to the floor below. Noise still echoed around us and hand-held lights still waved around on the catwalk above. Those searching were getting closer to the junction box I'd sabotaged. If they found it, could they repair the shield before help arrived? We needed our connection to the outside world to coordinate with our help when it arrived. Then I cut my speculation short as I heard a commotion from below, followed by the pounding of feet on the stairs.

I tapped Michelle and pointed down. She nodded. "You're all going to have to shut up now. Matt and I have to get off the stairs so I'm pocketing the comm."

Without another word, she pulled the comm from her ear and stuffed it in her pocket. Then she muttered, "Parents."

We went to the stair railing and Michelle climbed over the rail. "We're going to have to climb around the framework and hide behind the stairs."

I followed her example, adding, "You know heights terrify me."

"Yes, even if it wasn't in your briefing, I'd have figured it out watching you during that trip to the amusement park back in eighth grade." Michelle led the way along an extremely narrow girder, using one hand to steady herself with a girder just over her head. "I never did figure out why you rode the roller coaster so much, though. Didn't that scare you?"

I knew the chatter was Michelle's way of taking my mind off the yawning gulf below us, but I went along with it. Both of my hands gripped the girder above and I shuffled my feet, never picking them up from the girder below. "Roller coasters are the worst—until the coaster crests that first hill and the ride really gets started. Then they're the best thing ever."

Michelle reached a point beyond the stairs and casually stepped across a meter of open air to a girder behind the stairs. I reached the same point and froze, staring down to the docking bay floor far, far below us.

"Okay, babe, just take one big step and then we can just duck down in the shadows and let the pirates run right past us."

I nodded but my feet stubbornly stayed where they were while the pounding footsteps came closer and closer.

Michelle reached for me. "Just take my hand and step across, Matt. I know you can do it."

I reached toward her hand and then, hating myself, snatched my hand back to grab onto the girder above me. I whispered, "I'm sorry."

"You know it's bad luck to get your wife killed before you've even been married for a week, right?" Michelle gave up coaxing and shifted to a stern whisper. "Well, that's what will happen when those pirates see you standing over there. They'll shoot you and you'll fall. If I'm very lucky, the pirates will shoot me when they find me. Seeing how short of pretty women this base is, though, I'll probably end up as the plaything for a ship full of criminals."

"That's *not* going to happen," I whispered fiercely. Taking a deep breath, I stepped across to the next girder. I wobbled a bit, but Michelle steadied me.

"Great job, babe. Now we just have to sit down on the girder and we'll disappear into the shadows." Michelle gracefully straddled the girder, her feet dangling off either side of it. She patted her lap. "You can lean forward and lay your head in my lap. It'll be just like the night in the spaceship before we left Draconis."

Michelle held out a hand to steady me as I lowered myself onto the girder. With a shudder of relief, I leaned over and laid my head in her lap. Michelle gently stroked my hair as we huddled in the shadows. A moment later, feet pounded around the landing just below our position and up the stairs. We both held our breath, knowing this was when the pirates were most likely to spot us. They never even slowed down.

We waited for the pirates to ascend a few more flights of stairs before deciding it was safe to move. Before we got going, Michelle kissed me, smiled wickedly, and said, "You did really well, honey. So well you deserve something special in return."

"Like what?" I couldn't keep a bit of a leer off my face.

Michelle rose to her feet. "I'll tell you when we're back on the stairs."

Proper motivation is everything. I made it back to the stairs right behind Michelle and never once needed coaxing from her. Then she told me what her 'something special' was before leading off down the stairs.

"How am I supposed to concentrate on this mission after you planted *that* image in my mind?" I asked.

"That's easy, Matt. It won't happen until we get out of here and find ourselves a private room." Only then did she reach into her pocket and pull out the comm unit.

"Then let's get this over with."

We finished our descent without further incident but could no longer keep to the shadows. The floor of the docking bay around the two ships was brightly lit, providing illumination for the work being performed on the two pirate ships. Trying to act inconspicuous, we turned away from the two ships and toward the huge docking bay door.

Several pirates carried pads similar to Michelle's maintenance pad, so she pulled hers out and flashed it about. It's all about looking busy without actually being busy. It didn't work.

A pirate called, "Hey, you two. Can you help me over here?"

We needed to get the docking bay door open so Jonas's help could get inside and couldn't really spare time to help the pirate. But we also couldn't afford to rouse the man's suspicion. And, most importantly, we couldn't allow the pirate to get a look at Michelle. Just having the man watch her walk away, even wearing the loose and shapeless maintenance coveralls, was risky. If the clothes shifted at just the wrong moment, any man alive would recognize the feminine swing of Michelle's hips.

"I'll take care of this," I murmured. "You just keep walking away."

Not waiting for Michelle's answer, I spun about and headed toward the man who'd called. As subtly as possible, I put myself between Michelle's retreating form and the pirate. After all, the less he saw of her the better.

"What do you need?" I called.

"What I need is both of you." The pirate waved toward a portable machine mounted on a motorized cart. The right front of the cart rested on the floor, its wheel caught in the well for recessed rails. "The last moron to come through here with the crane didn't put the metal plate back over the tracks after he got past here."

At the far end of the first spaceship, a huge crane sat on the same set of rails. Near the stuck cart, a thin metal sheet lay on the floor.

"We've got a deadline, so you're going to have to settle for me. Just be glad the first part of our job can be done by one guy." I stopped beside the cart and adopted the standard 'guy studying a problem pose.' Basically, I crossed my arms and shook my head. "Man, you are stuck but good."

"Tell me something I don't know." The man wormed one end of a three meter piece of pipe between the lip of the recess for the rail and the front end of the cart. "Can you help me lever the wheel up and out?"

"Yeah, sure."

We were out in the plain sight of a bunch of other pirates, so I kept the stun stick up my sleeve. Instead, I grabbed the end of the pipe and the two of us put all of our weight onto it. The cart rose incredibly slowly out of the recess and, once clear, rolled backward onto level flooring. I released the pipe, ready to continue on my way, but noticed the pirate looking at my hands. A quick glance at his hands showed why. The man had some sort of spoked wheel tattooed on the back of his left hand.

Since I'd obviously seen him studying my hand, I had to say something. I thought of Cummings and Spitz. Did they have tattoos? I hoped not.

"I'm with Cummings' crew. We operate out in the open so we can't wear the mark."

The pirate nodded slowly. "Right. Sorry, but you can't be too careful."

"No problem. Look, I've got to catch up with my partner." I jerked a thumb over my shoulder in the direction Michelle went.

"Sure. Thanks for your help."

"No problem. See you around."

I turned and walked away, willing myself to act casually. I swore I could feel the man's eyes boring into my back and expected him to shout at any moment. Then I heard the obvious sounds of someone dragging a metal plate across the floor. A second later, I heard the whine of an electric motor and the clump-clump of wheels rolling over the metal plate. I heaved a big sigh of relief at my narrow escape.

Suddenly, the cart's little horn began beeping incessantly and the driver shouted, "We've got two intruders in the docking bay! Over here! Two intruders!"

I broke into a run, hoping to disappear into the shadows before too many pirates spotted me. It didn't take long to get out of the light, as the only well-lit areas were around the two ships. Once out of direct light, I steered clear of the pools of light around doors to storage areas and control boxes and the like. Behind me, the driver no longer shouted and the cart's horn no longer beeped.

That had to mean he'd drawn the attention he sought. How long did I have before pursuit swarmed all over this end of the docking bay?

Not long, it turned out. Shouts rose behind me and the sounds of a *lot* of running feet echoed around the docking bay. From far above, hand-held lights lanced down to the floor, forcing me to swerve and dodge even more. Staying in the shadows took so much of my attention, I feared I would miss the door controls entirely. Then I spotted something flashing dimly in the shadows to my left.

Risking discovery, I ignored the searching lights for a few seconds and stared hard at the flashing light. The light was too dim for a torch and too strangely shaped. It was rectangular and not more than thirty centimeters across. Then I got it—Michelle was waving the pad around so I could see the screen.

I put on a burst of speed to reach her—and the door controls —all the faster. And that's when one of the lights from far above caught me. I passed back into shadow in a fraction of a second, but I heard a shout from far above and half a dozen lights flicked to my area. I cut ninety degrees to the right and tried to angle around the sweeping lights. I mostly succeeded, but the pirates knew where I had been and the direction I had been running. Even if they never figured out my destination, the pirates had the manpower to find us with a simple brute force search.

I skidded to a stop at the door controls, just in time to help Michelle wrestle a metal barrel into place. She'd already dragged a few smaller boxes around the controls, creating some small cover.

"Matt, Daddy says to get the doors open fast. Help is on its way." Michelle angled the pad screen so it illuminated the keypad for the door controls. "He also sent a team of your bodyguards to the door in starship maintenance, but they won't be here for another two or three minutes."

"Got it." Never before had two or three minutes seemed like an eternity, but it sure did now. I pulled a range of tools out of the coverall pockets. "Did you have a chance to check out the keypad?"

"Yeah. They supported local business and stole a GenCo oh two oh one model."

I burst out laughing. "Seriously? That's the same model Jonas installed in my aunt and uncle's house after my parents disappeared."

"Why is that funny?"

My fingers tapped keys on the control pad. "I found out about the requisition before he filed it. That night, I used a backdoor into the GenCo system and installed a permanent code key into the keypad's firmware. I couldn't let a keypad keep me from slipping away from my bodyguards, after all."

"You mean you can open it?"

"Sure. It's a long code—I didn't want anyone stumbling across it by accident—but I'll have this thing open in twenty seconds."

Then two lights stabbed out of the darkness and lit the keypad and a man shouted, "They're at the door controls."

Michelle pulled me down behind her makeshift barrier as a hail of blaster bolts flashed all around us. "Duck, Matt!"

The barrier wasn't high enough to offer cover for the keypad. The keypad wasn't much higher, though. Surely, I could enter the code key without raising anything but my hand above the barrier. Without giving myself a chance for second thoughts, I reached for the keypad.

Blaster bolts spattered on the wall, showering us with hot sparks. Then pain erupted from my hand as a blaster bolt burned a hole in it down to the bone!

BREAKTHROUGH

I dropped to the floor, curling up around my throbbing hand. Much as I tried to stifle it, I screamed in pain.

"Oh my God, Matt!" Michelle spun around at my cry, fear and concern drawing her face taut. Her eyes searched for my wound and found nothing. "He's been shot, Daddy, but I can't see where."

I forced myself to unbend and showed her my right hand. She sucked breath in through her teeth when she saw the blaster burn. "No, it's not life-threatening, ma'am. He's got a hole burned halfway through his hand."

A hail of blaster bolts splattered against our makeshift barrier and the wall behind us. From what seemed like very far away, a pirate shouted, "Looks like we got the shooter. Move in!"

I waved Michelle back toward our defense. "You...shoot...I'm okay."

Concern still reflected on her face, Michelle nodded and spun around. She snapped off several shots and was rewarded with a scream from the other side. Shouts of surprise erupted and I heard the clatter of people scrambling for cover.

"Got one!" Michelle crowed. "That still leaves a few hundred, of course... Yes sir, Matt's wound *does* throw a spanner into Daddy's rescue plan."

Through the pain, the word 'spanner' triggered something. Spanner... Spanned... Hand... Rhyme time... Focus! I had to *span* the gap between cover and the keypad. I looked at the collection of tools I'd pulled from my tool belt. Heh, I did have a locking spanner. And the vibroblade hilt. Leaving the blade turned off, I clamped the spanner around the hilt and raised it to the keypad to continue tapping the code key. It came up just a few centimeters short.

"Dammit." I looked around for some way to make my code tapper a little longer—and spotted the stun stick and the roll of tape. Moving as quickly as my wounded hand allowed, hissing in agony throughout, I taped the spanner handle to the stun stick.

Michelle, hearing my oath, glanced quickly over her shoulder. "What are you doing? Keep your hand still or you'll make the wound worse."

"Keeping it still is more likely to make us dead," I said through gritted teeth. "We both know the pirates are just waiting until your power pack is exhausted. They'll be able to take us at their leisure once that happens. But I think I can use this to finish typing in the code key."

"How many more numbers do you have to enter?"

"I've already entered eight, so eight more." I lifted my extended code tapper with my left arm, struggling to keep it under control.

Michelle listened to her comm briefly. "Yes, Daddy, I was going to ask that...And what are the rest of the numbers, in case I have to enter them?"

"Your birthdate. The first eight are my birthdate." The vibroblade hilt wobbled too much to use one handed. Breathing fast, I grabbed the stun stick with my right hand, too. In my mind, I forced myself to imagine what would happen to Michelle if I didn't enter the code. Forcing that horrific image into a loop, I pushed the pain aside.

"You have *got* to be kidding me, Matt." Despite her incredulous tone, Michelle kept up her vigil, firing off a couple of shots. "You said you programmed that shortly after your parents disappeared."

I tapped the two digits for Michelle's birth month, fighting to keep from hitting any other keys. There wasn't time to do this twice, so it had to be right the first time. "I told you I've been in love with you since the sixth grade."

Tap.

Blaster fire picked up and bolts flew all around my makeshift tool. Michelle returned fire deliberately, conserving her power pack and trying to gain me time to finish the code. "Why don't the pirates just shoot the keypad? Won't that make it impossible for you to open the door?"

Tap.

"Yes, but it will make it impossible for them to open it, too. They've got to know the jig is up here at Pegasus Station." *Tap.* "Can you feel the deep thrumming that started up about the same time as our shootout?" *Tap.* "The pirates are powering up their ships. I'll bet they're going to make a run for it—but they can't run if they can't open the doors."

My control improved with each tap and I only two more numbers to go. Then a bolt caught the stun stick right below the spanner handle. With a crack, the stun stick broke.

"Son of a bitch!"

"Now what?" Michelle fired three more shots before looking over her shoulder. Seeing the broken stun stick in my hand, she simply said, "Oh."

"How many shots have you got left, babe?" I asked.

"Six or seven, maybe."

That didn't leave me time to tape the two pieces together, much less finish typing in the remaining two digits. I stared hard at the gap between our cover and the keypad. Never had half a meter seemed so far before.

Taking a deep breath, I said, "To hell with it. My hand is already wounded."

"Matt, what-"

Releasing my deep breath and fighting the pain, I raised my right hand to the keypad. The sharp smell of blaster fire against metal increased as the pirates shot faster. Two keys. I just needed to tap two keys. Then I could curl up around my shrieking hand again.

Tap.

I felt the heat of near misses and sharp prick of minor burns as sparks showered my hand.

Tap.

The door control light switched from red to green. Without giving myself a chance to think about it, I slapped my palm down on the door control. The jolt sent pain lancing from my hand and through my arm but then I felt the deep, metallic thump of doors releasing and the deeper hum of large motors pulling a heavy load.

"Matt did it!" Michelle called over the comm. "The doors are opening."

A pirate yelled, "Looks like we're out of time, boys, and the boss says hostages will come in handy. Let's get 'em!"

With a roar, half a hundred pirates rose from behind cover and charged our position.

I scooted up next to Michelle and we took turns firing around our metal barrel barricade. Michelle's blaster had much greater range and accuracy than my little taser—especially with me firing left handed—but the mass of charging pirates was hard to miss.

Just as I leaned out for my third shot, Michelle grabbed my coverall and pulled me to the ground. "Daddy says duck."

The high-pitched whine of repulsers came from our right, followed by the harsh glare and floor-melting heat of a ship-mounted laser cannon. Pirates screamed in pain and terror as another laser blast burned some of them and blinded a lot more. The mass of feet pounding toward our position became a rout of feet running away.

As I blinked my eyes to clear the after-image of laser bolts, I heard the whine of several more repulsers. In the dim light, the state-of-the-art starfighter hovering ten meters to our right shone like a beacon of hope on the darkest night of the year. Flight Commander Nancy Martin gave me a two-fingered salute, all the while barking out orders to her fighter wing. The five ships under her command maneuvered through the docking bay, harrying pirates and taking shots at the unshielded engine of the closer Q-ship.

Grinning from ear-to-ear at our sudden reversal of fortune, I said, "Michelle, tell Jonas we need a ride up to the catwalk so we can get my parents."

"Daddy already has that covered, Matt. Look." She pointed up at a small personnel shuttle hovering overhead. A team of armed men sprang from the shuttle to the catwalk and charged into the office.

"Once your parents are aboard, the shuttle will pick us up, too. Then we just wait for the Federation navy to arrive and mop up the pirates." Michelle took my uninjured left hand. "You did it, babe. You rescued your parents."

I gave Michelle a quick kiss, wishing we had time for a more leisurely one. "*We* did it, Michelle. I couldn't have done this without you."

Michelle's eyes danced as we watched the team hustle my parents out of their prison and onto the shuttle. She put the comm into my ear, saying, "Daddy wants to talk to you."

"Are you there, sir?"

"I married your daughter, Jonas. It's time to stop calling me sir."

"That might take a while, sir. Old habits die hard." Despite the formal tone, I heard the humor in Jonas's tone. "Once your parents are secure in the shuttle-"

An explosion rocked the docking bay, drowning out Jonas's next words. The remains of a starfighter rained down on the floor as the pirate ship furthest from the door rose ponderously from its docking cradle. A glowing laser barrel protruded from an open gun port. The ship's other lasers came to life, sweeping the docking bay firing at the darting starfighters.

Through the comm, I heard Jonas issuing orders over another comm. Despite all the noise and confusion, I still heard the hiss as Nancy opened the canopy of her starfighter. Her ship slid closer to us and she tossed a cloth pack our way.

"Put on the vacuum harnesses and then climb on top of my ship. You're coming out with me *right now*. I don't have room inside the cockpit, but the ship has lots of hand-holds and I'll be as gentle as possible."

We donned the harnesses and ran to the ship. Seeing me struggle to pull myself onto the fuselage, Michelle gave me a boost. "First thing when we're safe, we get that hand checked out, Matt."

"You'll get no arguments from me." I hooked my feet under a mechanic's hand-hold and gave Michelle a hand up with my uninjured left hand.

The two of us clung to the various hand-holds and each other, then Michelle gave our pilot a thumbs-up signal. With a metallic snap, Nancy closed her canopy and the starfighter rose into the air. Down the length of the docking bay, the other four remaining fighters twisted and turned, drawing fire and taking shots at the pirate ships. Above us, the shuttle carrying my parents banked and accelerated toward the huge bay doors, still in the process of grinding open.

Keeping her speed low and the fighter level, Nancy stayed close to the floor. I guess she hoped to remain unnoticed with everything else going on around her. The sudden explosion from the closer pirate ship's unshielded engine made sure no one had time to spare on a low flying fighter.

The pirate ship already under way continued its slow, stately drive down the long docking bay. Pirates from the other ship ran and waved and tried to board their sister ship. Showing the compassion one might expect from pirates, none on board the moving ship offered any help. Those who managed to climb a rope and reach an open hatch were allowed aboard. Cursing or shaking fists or pleading, the rest were abandoned to their fate.

Over the comm, Jonas ordered the rest of the fighters to cover our withdrawal and then make a run for it. "Your starfighters are no match for the pirate ship. Besides, you know the navy will want a piece of the action when they arrive."

Michelle squirmed close enough for our vacuum harness force-fields to overlap, allowing us to talk. "Just a few more minutes and this will all be over, Matt."

I grinned, gazing into her bright blue eyes. "I can't wait. Hey, maybe we can go on an actual honeymoon, too."

Michelle batted her eyes. "Won't you have to ask your wife, first?"

"Do you think that's a good idea? I've been assuming she'll give the okay."

Michelle's reply was lost when our starfighter flew from the docking bay—right into an ambush! A laser blast flashed just past the ship, narrowly missing Nancy's canopy. Michelle and I looked back and both of us gasped. GCS-1017—Cummings' ship—curved around Pegasus Station, the research vessel now showing itself as another Q-ship. More lasers flashed and the space around us turned from night to day.

In the cockpit, Nancy shouted something, which Jonas relayed immediately. "Hold on tight, sir. The gentle ride is over."

Even as I repeated that to Michelle, the starfighter rocketed forward. Both of us nearly lost our grips in that first burst, but we managed to hang on.

"Matt, once she puts a little range between you and Cummings' ship, your pilot plans to swing around to another docking bay and drop you off." Jonas's voice held more tension than I'd ever heard before. "You and Michelle just need to hold on for twenty seconds or so."

Once again, I started relaying the message to Michelle. I'd

gotten out three words when a laser blast hit the starfighter's port engine. The force of the blast and the loss of thrust from the port side threw the ship into a wild spin.

My good hand lost its grip, but my feet stayed firmly tucked under another hand-hold. The first buck threw Michelle's feet free and then her hands lost their grips. Her eyes wide in terror, Michelle tumbled away into deep space.

"No."

I didn't scream or shout. I whispered the word, but it carried all the love and loss a breaking heart could hold. All the while, I stared out into the depths of space, as if I might still see her.

"What is it, sir? What happened?"

"Michelle's gone, Jonas. She lost her grip and I couldn't catch her."

Jonas drew a ragged breath and I imagined him pulling his training around himself like a shield. He spoke in his usual, businesslike tone, but I heard the undertone of loss in his voice. "Did she have a comm unit or something else we can track?"

"Just the vacuum harness. She gave the comm to me."

"At my request." And there Jonas's control broke along with his voice.

"Isn't there any way we can find Michelle?" Mom asked.

"Without some kind of electronic broadcast signal, there's nothing we can do, dear." Dad spoke in the same matter-of-fact tone he used when I was a boy. I knew he felt the loss, but you could never tell from his voice.

Without conscious thought, I pulled my feet from under the hand-hold and, as the ship swung into a turn, pushed away from Nancy's starfighter. The little ship vanished into the distance in seconds as I floated in the void.

Back toward Pegasus Station, lasers flashed and seared holes in ships' hulls. The hulking pirate Q-ship nosed out of the secret docking bay, all gun ports open and laser fire spitting from every gun. Cummings' ship flew ahead, clearing a path for its still-ponderous sister ship. I assumed starfighters buzzed around the larger ships, but I was too far away to see them. And I didn't care about them, anyway.

I turned my gaze out to the depths of space and fought against my emotions, trying to clear my mind.

"Sir? What have you done?" Jonas was back in control of himself. "Your comm signal isn't with the starfighter anymore."

"I'm going to look for Michelle," I said. "Follow my comm signal and pick me up with the shuttle. We'll need it when I find her."

"Find her? But sir-"

"Hush Jonas," Mom said. "Let him concentrate."

To my surprise, the comm fell silent. I stared out into the black and shoved everything that wasn't Michelle from my mind. I remembered her look, her feel, her scent, her sound, her grace, her humor. I remembered *her* and she filled my mind and consumed my senses. She filled me as no one ever could. I only had to find the spark, the emotion, the source of all that I held in my mind. And I couldn't do it.

I saw the bright sparks which were my parents. I saw, back on Pegasus Station, a third spark. Dim and barely perceptible, just like when Michelle and I reached the pirate docking bay. But I couldn't see Michelle. I couldn't see anyone else. It was like a wall blocked me from seeing more—a wall I couldn't break.

In frustration, I pounded my head with my fists and fed on the pain. I could *not* fail. I could *not* lose Michelle. I would *not* fail.

Through the pain and the pounding of my fists, through my rage and ranting, an image rose. Michelle and me on the floor of the *M&M*, her hands holding my head, her eyes closed, her mouth hungrily kissing me, her breath warm on my face.

Read me now.

I charged at my mental wall, borne by the strength of Michelle's love, and it shattered before our combined might. I stood beyond the ruins of the wall and vast waves of emotions crashed down upon me. Instinctively, I fell back from the onslaught. Instinctively, I went to hide behind my wall.

No! If I retreated behind the wall, I knew I'd never break through it again. If I retreated behind the wall, I'd lose Michelle forever. I forced myself to turn into the face of the emotional tidal wave.

"There's too much! How can I find her through it all?"

"Find her through all *what*?" Jonas asked.

"Through everyone. They're all there and I don't know how to get rid of them."

"Matt, honey, do you mean your ability?" Mom and Dad always called it that. I guess it was safer than calling me an empath.

"I broke through the wall, Mom, but there's so much out there."

Dad and Jonas began speaking, offering confusing and contradictory suggestions before Mom cut them off. "Shut up, both of you and let me help my son find Michelle."

The emotions of half a million people continued hammering at my mind and I was beginning to lose myself in them. I felt my grip on sanity weakening.

"Help me, Mom. I don't know how long I can hold on."

"Be my brave boy, son, just like when you were little and afraid of the dark. Concentrate on the sound of my voice." Mom hummed a few bars from the lullaby she used to sing to me. "Now, can you identify different emotions? Like fear? I'm sure Michelle is scared right now."

Fear was easy. It felt like everyone in the solar system was afraid of something right then. But I concentrated on the fear and the torrent of emotions ebbed slightly.

"Yes. But there's a lot of fear, Mom. I still can't pick Michelle out of all of that."

"I know, baby. That's just the start. Now, can you filter through all those frightened people for the ones feeling love? Michelle loves you and she has to be feeling that love even as she feels fear."

I opened myself to love slowly, careful to hold the fear filter in place. I managed to push aside more sparks of emotion. "Okay, got it, Mom. What next?"

"Sorrow. Michelle must certainly be feeling that."

With each additional filter, I got better at holding the others and adding a new one. And Mom guided me to filter for compassion and then for feelings of loss. But hundreds of emotional sparks still burned, washing out any hope I could pick a single one from among them.

"What else, Mom? I still can't pick her out."

"Now add you."

"Me? I'm not an emotion, Mom."

"You are to Michelle. You are love and life and joy and passion and laughter and sorrow and everything that makes her life worth living."

The shuttle slid up next to me as I added one last filter in my mind. Far away, in the normal universe, an airlock opened and my father floated toward me, a tether line stretching back to the shuttle. Dad caught hold of me and used the tether to pull us back to the airlock. As air hissed back into the chamber, my final filter fell into place.

And there she was. Michelle, glowing with fear and love and sorrow and compassion—and all for *me*!

Dad pulled me into the shuttle's cabin.

"I've got her, Mom. I found her!"

My mother wrapped me in a hug. "I knew you could do it, son. Just point the way and we'll go get her."

Mom relayed my directions to Dad, who relayed them to the shuttle pilot. The rest of the rescue team just sat and watched us. Somewhere in the back of my mind, I wondered if we'd have to pay these men to keep quiet about my ability, because there was no hiding it from them.

Six minutes after Dad pulled me into the shuttle, I went back out for Michelle. As I caught her in my arms, I said, "I was afraid I'd lost you forever, Michelle."

Wrapping her arms tightly around me, Michelle rested her head on my shoulder. "Silly boy, I knew you'd find me."

As Dad reeled us in, I put the comm unit into Michelle's ear.

"Hi Daddy...No, I'm fine...Really, Daddy...I love you, too."

I held onto my wife all the way back to Pegasus Station.

TERRIBLE CHOICES

The emotional pressure on my mind increased the closer the shuttle came to the teeming population of Pegasus Station. The filters I used to find Michelle slipped and slid the longer I held them in place. I struggled to put the filters back in place, to find the same serenity I'd found floating in the void. All the while, I clutched Michelle tighter, as if she were a lifeline and I was a drowning man—which I was, in a way.

Michelle sensed my conflict and pulled my head onto her shoulder. Stroking my hair, she whispered comforting nothings into my ear. I breathed deeply, concentrating on her scent and her sound. Together we held the emotions at bay, but only barely. If my filters fell or if I let go of Michelle, the battering emotions would overwhelm me.

Barely on the edge of my perception, I heard Dad speaking to Jonas over the shuttle's comm. "The pilot put the station between us and the fighting. What's the situation out there, Jonas?"

"The two pirate ships are clear of the station, but their course doesn't make any sense, Richard. Instead of running for the wormhole, they're diving toward the sun."

"Is the Federation Navy in the system?"

"Unless a patrol just happens to swing by, we can't expect a naval response for at least another six hours. The ship carrying our message is still in the wormhole to Eridani Station."

Michelle broke off her whispers to me. "There's an uncharted wormhole close to the sun. It takes you to the middle of nowhere, but there's another uncharted wormhole from there to Rockville Station."

"How did you learn about that, pumpkin?"

"Matt and I came through those wormholes when we were running from Rockville Station."

"The two of you went to Rockville station by yourselves?" Dad asked. "Mining stations like Rockville can be kind of rough if you're not careful."

"Did you hear that, Matt?" Michelle's laugh had a tinge of hysteria to it. My laugh sounded downright insane to my ears. "You might want to have the family lawyers contact Rockville Station on behalf of Matt and me."

"You'd better brief us, Michelle." Jonas was all business again.

"No, Jonas, she will do no such thing." Mom's tone said the topic was not open to discussion. "Your daughter and our son have been through a lot. What happened on Rockville Station can wait until they've rested and had some time to themselves."

"We're going to need more than that, ma'am," Michelle said. "Matt's struggling with something—all the emotions, I guess."

"God, how stupid of me. I should have realized that." I felt Mom sit next to me and put a hand on my back.

"You've had a lot going on, also, ma'am."

"Michelle, stop calling me ma'am. You're family now. I'm Angela. Or Mom, if you wish." I felt Mom slip out of her seat to kneel before me. She took my head in her hands. "Look at me, son."

It took all my willpower to turn away from Michelle and meet Mom's gaze. Her eyes held the same love and concern I'd seen a thousand times before.

"Can you drop your filters and read me, son?"

"I don't know. There's so much pressure built up outside the filters, I might not be able to switch from Michelle to you fast enough."

"Sure you can, Matt. You've read me thousands of times. This is no different. You just let go of one person and catch hold of another. You can do it, honey. Trust me. Trust yourself."

I took a deep breath, released it, and dropped my filters at the same time. A flood of emotions swept over me. Instinctively, I flinched away from it all, away from Mom, but she held tight to my head and forced me to look into her eyes. I scrambled to catch her emotions and use them to pull myself from the flood from Pegasus Station. One by one, I caught her feelings—love, compassion, concern, and...shame? I almost lost our connection when shame surfaced, but kept hold of it.

"Good, Matt. Just hold on to all of that. Now, without letting go of our connection, blank your mind. Imagine a pure white sheet of paper or maybe pure darkness."

I remembered the deep black of space I experienced twenty minutes and a lifetime ago. I drew the dark emptiness of space around me like a cloak. As the cloak of darkness settled over my mind, flashing emotions flickered and vanished, leaving a small starscape of lights I never wanted to lose—Michelle, Mom, Dad, and even a dim spark that was Jonas. Plus that other spark I'd seen before.

I felt my tension ebb and smiled at the two most important women in my life. And I realized my burned hand no longer hurt. Sometime during my struggle to block out the emotions, the rescue team's medic numbed my hand and covered it with a Second Skin patch—manufactured by GenCo, of course.

"Mom, how did you know how to guide me through all of this?"

"I knew you had powerful potential, Matt. I felt it while you were still in my womb." Mom looked down, unwilling to meet my eyes. "My range is only a few meters, but the principles are the same."

"Why didn't you tell me? And why didn't you teach me?"

"Your father and I were afraid we'd lose you. Even with my

minor powers, I came close to giving myself away half a dozen times during puberty. With your greater power..." Mom looked up, her eyes bright with tears. "We just hoped you'd never test yourself beyond what little you did by instinct."

With a soft clump, the shuttle settled into a docking bay. The hatch cycled and Jonas charged in. He dropped to his knees and pulled his daughter into a tight hug.

Mom watched father and daughter, smiling. "I'm sorry. I should have given you what little training I could."

"Yeah, it would have made finding you and Dad a lot easier. But when it really mattered, when Michelle's life was on the line, you did train me."

Suddenly, Jonas's right arm wrapped around me and he pulled me into his hug with Michelle. "Sir...Matt...Thank you for saving my girl."

"I love her, Jonas."

"That's nothing new, Matt. You've loved Michelle for years."

Michelle pulled back from her father. "You *knew* and you never told me?"

"Pumpkin, what happens to fathers who meddle in their daughter's love lives?" Michelle opened her mouth to reply, then closed it again. Jonas nodded. "Exactly. You just have to learn some things on your own."

Dad motioned us all to exit the shuttle. "I'm sure we have a lot to discuss, but we can do that later. Let's get off this shuttle and see about getting home to Draconis."

"Jonas, did station traffic control stop all ship departures? I asked.

"With a battle going on around the station? Of course. Now that it's moved toward the sun, though, they'll probably open things up soon."

"No, tell them to hold departures a while longer."

"Oh, right," Michelle said, "we've got to make sure Hector's ship doesn't get away."

"Who is Hector?" Dad asked.

"He's part of that long Rockville Station story," I said. "But that's not the only reason I want all ships held."

That dim, unknown spark was no longer dim—and no longer unknown.

I looked over my shoulder at Michelle's father. "Jonas, you and the team stay with my parents. Keep them safe and alert security about everything that's happened."

"What is your plan, sir?" Jonas asked, his eyes hard upon me.

"I've got one more thing to do before we can wrap up this whole affair." I flashed a quick smile at Jonas and caught Michelle's hand. "I'll even take one of my bodyguards with me."

Jonas and my parents watched me lead Michelle away and none of them tried to stop us.

Once we rounded a corner and were out of sight of our parents, Michelle put a soft hand against my cheek and turned my head to face her. "What's going on, Matt?"

"I'm going to confront the person behind my parents' kidnapping."

"Cummings is on his ship, so you can't mean him. And you've already confronted Hector—help me remember to send a security team to pick him up." Michelle bit her lip. "Is it Arthur Jewel, the guy in traffic control?"

"No. Please just let me handle this my way."

"Sorry, but I can't do that." Michelle pulled me to a stop. "We're not just rich kid Matt and bodyguard Michelle any more. In the eyes of God and the law, we are one. If you lie to me, you lie to yourself. If you hide something from me, you hide it from yourself."

"All right, I'll tell you." I resumed walking and Michelle slipped her hand free and wrapped it around my waist. Drawing support from her touch, I said, "I picked up someone besides my parents when we entered the pirate docking bay."

"Maybe it was someone having a big emotional spike?"

"That's what I thought at the time, but the spark was there again when my powers broke free. This time, it didn't go away and was still there after Mom helped me control things." I sighed. "And that's when I managed to identify who was behind that dim spark."

I walked in silence for a few seconds. Michelle quietly watched me, giving me time to find the right words. In the end, I found no words and just blurted it out.

"It's Aunt Tess." My voice cracked as I said it.

Michelle's arm tightened around me as her surprise and concern washed over me. "You're sure?"

I nodded, my eyes filling with tears. "She's been like a mother to me since my parents disappeared. Her emotions were always vague, much harder to read than my parents, but I know she loves me. And I simply cannot reconcile that love with the pain she caused."

"Could her presence here just be a coincidence? She could simply be here for business."

I shook my head. "The first time I picked her up, after we left that elevator room, she was on the floor of the pirate docking bay, somewhere between us and my parents."

"Oh."

After that, we walked in silence to the docking bay reserved for small ships. Crew and passengers of the ships milled about, speculating nervously about pirates and raging space battles. Seeing our maintenance coveralls, a few people tried to pump us for information. Michelle and I always shrugged and feigned ignorance.

Before long, we stood outside the airlock to a private ship. Unlike all the others, no crew or passengers stood outside.

I turned to face Michelle and gazed into her eyes. "Can you give me a few minutes alone with her? I have to give her a chance to explain herself—just her and me."

Once again biting her lip, Michelle nodded. "You've got five minutes, then I'm calling security and coming in after you."

I kissed her on the forehead, turned and opened the airlock, then entered Aunt Tess's ship. No one met me. No crew bustled about performing prelaunch checks. The ship was so silent my footsteps echoed through the corridors.

I felt the familiar spark to my left and turned that way. Ten seconds later, I entered a small, well-appointed ship's lounge. Aunt Tess reclined in a chair against the far wall.

She smiled sadly, unshed tears glistening in her eyes. "Hello, Matt. I can't tell you how happy I am to see you safe. How did you escape from those kidnappers?"

"Hello Aunt Tess." I returned her sad smile. "We both know there were never any kidnappers. That was just a story to cover my search for my parents." I couldn't keep bitter recrimination out of my voice. "You know, your brother and sister-in-law?"

"Don't you take that tone with me, young man." Aunt Tess tried for the same tone Mom used on me when I was little. "I know very well who your parents are."

"Just as you knew exactly *where* my parents were all the time I lived with you." I released the emotions I'd held in check and anger blazed forth. "So don't you *dare* take a maternal tone with me. You no longer have that right."

My aunt sprang to her feet, her hand swinging to slap me. "Ungrateful boy! I did what *had* to be done to save our company, our family, and our position in society."

I caught Aunt Tess's hand and held it firm. "Strange how you saved your family by sacrificing mine."

Aunt Tess tugged her arm back, but I tightened my grip. "You're hurting me, Matt."

"It's nothing like the pain you've inflicted on me for the last seven years."

"Do you think I *enjoyed* doing what I did? It nearly broke me having your parents taken from you." Tears streamed down my aunt's face. "I made a horrible choice, but all the other choices were worse."

I released Aunt Tess's arm and gently pushed her back into her chair. "Short of killing my parents, how could any choice be worse than having them kidnapped and held prisoner for years?"

"You know so little of the situation, Matt. Do you have any

idea what revealing the Pegasus Station pirate base would do to GenCo?"

"I don't know and I don't care."

"According to Cummings, that's exactly what your father said when he discovered the base all those years ago. Damn the man and his quest for efficiency. In a hundred years, no one ever bothered to analyze Pegasus Station's power usage—until Richard paid a visit seven years ago." Aunt Tess blew out an exasperated breath. "He turned up power usage he couldn't explain and set out to discover what happened to the excess power. If Richard had simply talked to Gunther and me, we could have steered him away from this."

"Uncle Gunther is in on this, too?"

"In on it? My dear boy, Gunther was one of the pirates when I met him. You know how it is with good girls and bad boys. I was smitten and the pirates liked the idea of putting one of their own on the board of GenCo."

I tried to keep the surprise off of my face and failed completely. Aunt Tess noted my expression and kept going.

"But because of your meddling—"

"Rescuing my parents from pirates is *not* meddling."

"We're just going to have to agree to disagree on that one, Matt. But that's neither here nor there. You've forced our hand. Gunther and I must start new lives somewhere else in the galaxy. If you wanted to cause me pain, son, you've succeeded."

"You're breaking my heart, Aunt Tess. And you're not getting away so easily. Security is on their way to arrest you even as we speak."

"How amusing. Do you think something as simple as a hold on departures will stop me from leaving? Docking clamps and station tractor beams aren't strong enough to hold a ship. We'll just ignore the hold and leave."

"We?"

A gruff, male voice spoke behind me. "Yes, we."

I spun to find Hector standing behind me, a blaster trained on my chest.

"Tess. Me." A fierce, predatory grin spread across his face. "And you."

Why was I surprised to find Hector backing up my aunt? As high ranking members of the gang, they had to know each other. But somehow, I never expected Aunt Tess to sink so low and to associate with someone like Hector. What was she thinking?

And then I realized I'd asked the wrong question of myself. I had to know what she was *feeling*. Pretending I was shocked into inaction, I concentrated on Aunt Tess's emotions. I had trouble letting her emotions in while keeping everybody on Pegasus Station out. Making the connection took such concentration, I lost track of everyone else—even my parents and Michelle. In the end, my emotional world shrank to Tess and me.

My aunt's emotions were like a thin sheet of glass—brittle—and I was a little boy with a handful of stones.

"You've certainly lowered your standards, Aunt Tess. I can see the value of a thug like Hector, but I can't believe you tracked him down and freed the man after I tazed him." It was time to give her an emotional smack down. I turned a look of scorn on her. "Or is your relationship with Hector more than just business? Are you bored with Gunther? Did you find Hector's uncouth swagger appealing? Tell me, Aunt Tess, did you run to his rescue, heart all aflutter? Is he your–"

Aunt Tess surged back to her feet and this time I didn't block her hand as it slapped my cheek. "How dare you make such insinuations! If your uncle was here he'd beat you within an inch of your life."

"Well, good old Uncle Gunther isn't here—but you've got the next best thing. Hector over there is just chomping at the bit to beat me to death." I glanced over my shoulder at the man. "Isn't that right, Hector?"

An inarticulate growl rose in Hector's throat. He kept the blaster leveled at my chest, but took a step in my direction.

"That's enough, both of you."

As Aunt Tess spoke, I felt something hard and dark slide over her emotions. I'd never felt anything like it, but recognized it immediately. It was a mental fortress, a wall to guard her emotions while she did unspeakable things.

"Matthew, you have one chance to stop acting like a spoiled child. You cannot provoke me into doing something foolish." Her eyes narrowed. "But you can convince me that saving you isn't worth my time and trouble. In which case I'll let Hector have his way with you."

Some of my surprise must have leaked through my expression, because Aunt Tess smiled sharply and said, "Of course I love you, child, but this is a harsh business. I must weigh the benefits of my love against the benefits of sacrificing that love. I did the same thing with your parents. Cooperate with me and I can promise you'll be comfortable. You may even come to enjoy our life."

"I could never enjoy such a life."

"Really? I think two or three beautiful young women at your beck and call, ready to satisfy your every desire—and young men have so *many* desires—might change your mind." My aunt regarded me thoughtfully. "If you behave yourself, we might even let you go along on raids and claim any young woman who catches your fancy."

I didn't even try to keep the revulsion off my face. "You're trying to bribe me with slave girls? Are there no depths to which you won't sink? Why would any sane man want a harem of terrified, unwilling women when he could find his soulmate and spend his life with her?"

"Oh dear, have you become infatuated with that little blonde girl you ran off with?" Aunt Tess tutted and shook her head in disapproval. "She's not good enough for you, Matt. After all, you're a Connaught. She's just a bodyguard, hardly better than a servant."

It was my turn to smile sharply. "No, Aunt Tess, she's my wife."

Aunt Tess's eyes widened. "Your wife? What-"

As if on cue, Michelle's voice echoed down the hallway, interrupting my aunt. "Matt, turn on Nancy's gift to you."

Nancy's gift? What did Michelle mean? Then I remember Flight Commander Nancy Martin tossing two vacuum harnesses to us. I'd completely forgotten I still wore the thing. Once on board the shuttle, I turned it off but was too busy holding Michelle to take it off.

Aunt Tess frowned at Hector. "I told you to lock the hatch after Matt came aboard."

Hector growled, "I had other stuff to do. Don't sweat it, though. I'll go get the girl."

The deck beneath our feet gave a lurch. All three of us recognized it as a docking tractor beam reversing to push a ship free of its berth. Immediately, a klaxon sounded, followed by a dispassionate voice.

"*Warning. Airlock open. Warning. Vacuum conditions imminent.*"

Hector spat a curse and started down the corridor toward the airlock. I flipped on my vacuum harness. Aunt Tess, eyes wide, stared at me. I expected her to ask for help, for me to hold her and let my harness's atmosphere shield extend to envelope her, too.

"What do you mean, that girl is your *wife?*" She spoke sharply, disbelief warring with surprise as she voiced the comment Michelle interrupted. Her rising voice carried, even over the klaxon. "Matthew Bernard Connaught, how could you do something so stupid?"

I wrapped my right arm around a permanent wall fixture. "Oh, that's not the half of it, auntie dear." I leaned toward her, my face mere centimeters from hers. "We did *not* sign a prenuptial agreement."

Aunt Tess's hand flew to her mouth as a truly shocked expression settled over her face. "You young idiot-"

Then the ship drifted clear of the docking bay's atmosphere shield. With the roar of wind, the ship's air supply rushed out of the airlock. The rushing wind caught Aunt Tess in mid-protest and swept her toward the airlock. She flailed for a handhold, bounced off the far wall, and was sucked into the corridor. Pulled horizontal by the depressurization, I wrapped my left hand around the fixture and held on.

In seconds, the roaring eased and then vanished entirely. I dropped from horizontal back to the deck, banging my knees against the bulkhead. I rose to my feet slowly and turned toward the exit—just in time to catch Michelle as she ran into my arms.

"I was so afraid Hector would just shoot you!" Her lips pressed against mine before I could answer.

I finished the kiss and pulled back a bit. "What happened to Hector and Aunt Tess?"

"They went out the airlock." Something must have shown on my face, because Michelle hastened to add, "Don't worry, they got blown back inside the station's atmosphere shield. Unless they do something stupid, they'll be fine."

"Have I told you that you are the most amazing woman ever? How did you get inside the ship? Hector said he locked the hatch."

Michelle ducked her head, her cheeks coloring slightly. "I snuck in behind you and hid in the compartment across from the airlock. I had to be close enough to help if anything went wrong."

"You mean like Hector coming up behind me with a blaster?"

"Yeah, something exactly like that."

"Well, that's okay then." I smiled and kissed Michelle again. "Should we dock this ship before it becomes a navigation hazard?"

Arms around each other, we went to the bridge. By the time I figured out the necessary controls, security had picked up Hector and Aunt Tess. I gently nudged the ship back to the dock, letting the docking tractor beams handle everything once the ship was in range.

I took Michelle's hand and we walked off the ship and into the arms of our waiting family.

EPILOGUE

You know what the problem is with adventures? The boring wrap-up—including all the annoying paperwork—takes far longer than the exciting part. In a properly run galaxy, the Federation Navy would show up just in time to catch the pirates, Michelle and I would thank everyone who helped us, and then my family would return home to live happily ever after.

If only...

A Federation Navy squadron arrived an hour and a half after the two pirate ships jumped out of the system through the wormhole near the sun. According to reports, ten hours after leaving the Pegasus system, the two ships took the charted wormhole away from Rockville Station. From there, they blended into regular traffic patterns and vanished. No doubt they'll set up shop somewhere else, but I'll let the navy worry about that. Pirate hunting never was my goal.

The pirates left behind in the Pegasus Station pirate base, finding the elevator room exit blocked by one of Jonas's teams, grabbed vacuum harnesses and swarmed through the spaceship exit. They fought their way to a freight docking bay, grabbed one of the docked freighters, and made a hard burn after their fellow pirates. In their desperation, the pirates forgot that all three of

Pegasus Station's starfighter wings harried the two Q-ships all the way to the wormhole. The starfighters intercepted the stolen freighter near the sun. Unlike the heavily armed Q-ships, the stolen ship only mounted light weapons. In minutes, the starfighters reduced the freighter to a drifting wreck. The wreck plunged into the sun long before rescue ships could reach it.

Once on the scene, the Feds fired off high-speed messenger drones with an arrest warrant and Psi Corps interrogation orders for Uncle Gunther. The pirate messenger drones must have gotten there faster. Uncle Gunther vanished hours before Federation agents came to arrest him, cleaning out quite a few bank accounts along the way. The Feds assume he's returned to the pirates, but I'm not so sure. Uncle Gunther does love Aunt Tess and I believe he's concocting a plan to spring her from Federation custody. But, again, that's a problem for the Feds.

Aunt Tess refused to talk, of course, but such a high profile prisoner in such a high profile case warranted special attention. The Feds brought in their top telepath to drag the information out of her—and verify the stories the rest of us gave. How could a telepath fail to discover my powers? How could I face involuntary induction into Psi Corps right after marrying the woman I love and reuniting with my parents?

Once again, Mom was there for us. She did a lot of research into empathic powers after I was born. Apparently, empaths and telepaths mix about as well and oil and water. Telepathy is all about conscious thoughts while empathy is all about unconscious emotions. Each tends to muddle the other. In practical terms, a telepath can only tell if an empath's statements are true or false. *And* an empath can 'cover' someone he truly cares about if he's touching them during the interrogation. As Michelle's husband, I had the right to be present during her questioning, as did Mom with Dad. With Mom and me masking Michelle's and Dad's stray thoughts, the telepath could only verify the truth of their statements. Since that was the only thing expected of the telepath, we simply told the truth and passed with flying colors.

Aunt Tess, on the other hand, fought the telepath every step of the way. But the telepath dragged the whole story—including our family history with the pirates—out of her. The procedure is agonizing. It took all of my concentration to block Aunt Tess's suffering out of my mind. Painful as that was, it paled compared to the story dragged from her mind.

In the early days of Pegasus Station, my great grandfather struggled to keep the station operating while waiting for traffic to grow. Desperate for funds, he and Hector's grandfather, Pedro, who faced a similar problem with his Redshift Mining Company, formed the pirate company. Using the wormholes Pedro discovered, their pirates robbed miners—including Redshift miners. Pedro collected insurance money for the lost ore *and* split the profits when Great Granddad fenced the ore through Pegasus Station.

The two of them ran a tidy little business, right up until my grandfather was born. By then, both companies were on firm footing and growing. Great Granddad proposed disbanding the gang. Pedro didn't like that idea. Then Great Granddad was killed in an accident, leaving Pedro in complete control of the gang. None of Great Granddad's children ever even knew about the pirates. Aunt Tess suspects Pedro had Great Granddad murdered, which is why she insisted the pirates keep Mom and Dad prisoner rather than kill them. I guess Aunt Tess told the truth when she called the kidnapping a horrible decision taken instead of worse choices. Of course, telling my parents the truth about the pirates never occurred to her.

When Dad and Aunt Tess were in college, my grandfather put them into low level company jobs for a few months. They lived under assumed names and had to support themselves entirely on their salary. The plan was to give them an idea of the life of the average worker in the company. Dad ended up in a factory on Mars and thrived. Tess got stuck in an office on Pegasus Station, where she badly mismanaged her money. Granddad sent Tess some money—the amount you'd expect a middle class father to send to his cash-strapped daughter—but Tess always had expensive tastes. She found her way to a loan shark and used her real name to try to land a big loan. That's when Gunther stepped in. The real irony is that Granddad was proud of his daughter for finding such an intelligent, ambitious young man and proud of his new son-in-law for his work ethic. I expect the truth will crush my grandfather when he hears it.

On behalf of those who helped on Pegasus Station, I submitted a claim for the reward for rescuing my parents. The company holding the reward policy granted them partial credit for the rescue and a share of the reward. Greg and Nora each got ten percent and assured me they could live quite comfortably on twenty-five million credits. To their astonishment, Nancy and her team were awarded one percent each, with smaller awards going to the other two flights and all the dock workers who rallied to Michelle's aid when Hector's men threatened us.

GenCo stock tanked when the pirate story broke. More than a few fortunes crumbled as a result. My family lost half of our wealth and my parents dedicated half of what was left to making some kind of restitution to the victims of the pirates. That still leaves us with over twenty billion credits, so we aren't exactly destitute. The rest of the GenCo board isn't happy with us—and me in particular —for screwing up the status quo. On the other hand, our desire to make things right struck a chord with the general public. Dad says GenCo will survive the scandal and emerge stronger in the end.

When we finally returned to Draconis, our parents insisted Michelle and I have what Mom called a Real Wedding. Being a guy, I didn't see the point, but Michelle embraced the idea. It's amazing how quickly a wedding can come together if you throw enough money at it. Just six weeks after our first wedding, I stood in the same cathedral which held my parents' premature memorial service and watched Jonas escort Michelle down the aisle. In that moment, seeing Michelle's bright eyes and dazzling smile, I understood why our parents wanted this.

Before, on Pegasus Station, Michelle and I proclaimed our love before God and each other. Now, we proclaimed our love before our family and friends. Before, we gave our vows in private. Now, we presented them for the galaxy to witness. Then we had our kiss at the end of the ceremony.

Just as our lips touched, Michelle breathed, "Read me now."

THE STORY CONTINUES...

Matt's and Michelle's story continues in *The Fugitive Pair*.
Available now!

If you enjoyed *The Fugitive Heir*, please post a brief review.
Reader recommendations are the best advertising.

ABOUT THE AUTHOR

Growing up, Henry worked at the usual range of menial jobs before ending up in software development. In between the menial jobs and the IT jobs, he achieved some small fame as the writer and co-creator of the small press comic book titles Southern Knights and X-Thieves. In 2006, Henry also took up the mantle of professional storyteller. He performs regularly throughout the state of North Carolina and has recently released his first book of children's stories.

Henry has been a fan of science fiction for as long as he can remember. He has loved space opera and planetary romance since the beginning, that is why his science fiction novels end up in those subgenres.

Henry currently lives in Raleigh, NC, with his wife, son, two cats, and lots of imaginary friends all clamoring to tell him of their adventures.

www.henryvogelwrites.com

ALSO BY HENRY VOGEL

www.ingramcontent.com/pod-product-compliance
Lightning Source LLC
Chambersburg PA
CBHW030312200626
46816CB00002BA/864